Seducing Lily Would Certainly Be No Hardship.

Convincing her, now that would be the challenge, and there was nothing in life that Hunter loved more than a challenge.

Was that fear he had detected in her voice? Hunter knew he should feel some sense of compassion for her, but it was a commodity he was very short on when it came to the Fontaines. Yes, he knew her secrets, knew all about her fall from grace. It couldn't have worked better if he'd planned it himself.

Dear Reader,

I think most people have a deep sense of pride for the part of the world in which they live, and we Kiwis are no different. When you live in a country that offers so much unspoiled and untamed beauty you're entitled to be proud.

The peninsula upon which I've set *Tycoon's Valentine Vendetta* is imaginary, but the real New Zealand coastline is also dotted with fingers of land reaching into the sea lined with glorious white sand beaches. Water sports are big here and we have the highest boat ownership per capita in the world!

I hope you enjoy this slice of New Zealand while reading about Jack and Lily's rocky reunion. Like many of my stories, this one has gone through several transformations before being brought to you in this format. To me, that's the beauty of telling stories for a living—you get to change and rework things until they're just right.

With best wishes from,

Yvonne

YVONNE
LINDSAY

TYCOON'S VALENTINE VENDETTA

Silhouette®
Desire

Published by Silhouette Books
America's Publisher of Contemporary Romance

ISBN-13: 978-0-373-76854-7
ISBN-10: 0-373-76854-0

TYCOON'S VALENTINE VENDETTA

This edition published by arrangement with Harlequin Books S.A.

Visit Silhouette Books at www.eHarlequin.com

Printed in U.S.A.

Books by Yvonne Lindsay

Silhouette Desire

The Boss's Christmas Seduction #1758
The CEO's Contract Bride #1776
The Tycoon's Hidden Heir #1788
Rosselini's Revenge Affair #1811
Tycoon's Valentine Vendetta #1854

*New Zealand Knights

YVONNE LINDSAY

New Zealand born to Dutch immigrant parents, Yvonne Lindsay became an avid romance reader at the age of thirteen. Now, married to her blind date and with two surprisingly amenable teenagers, she remains a firm believer in the power of romance. Yvonne feels privileged to be able to bring to her readers the stories of her heart. In her spare time, when not writing, she can be found with her nose firmly in a book, reliving the power of love in all walks of life. She can be contacted via her Web site, www.yvonnelindsay.com.

Jessica, this one's for you, with grateful thanks for all your patience and guidance, and your cleverness in drawing the best out of my characters and me. Working with you isn't work at all.

One

An icy blade streaked through every cell in Lily Fontaine's body. The fine hair on the back of her neck rose with a chill of foreboding that had nothing to do with the afternoon sea breeze rolling in off the beach.

He was here.

It had always been that way between them—that immediate awareness, the instant connection. Five minutes into her first foray back to her hometown of Onemata, New Zealand, in nearly ten years and it appeared little had changed. The same electricity crackled between them. She knew she had to face him, this ghost from her past—a past she'd been running from for so long and so hard it had finally brought her full circle. She lifted her eyes, compelled to seek confirmation even though she knew without doubt he was within a couple of metres of her right now.

And there he was. Jack Dolan. Her first love. Her last.

A waft of expensive cologne filtered past her, overriding the scent of petrol fumes on the service station forecourt as surely as he'd overwhelmed her with his passion and eventually his indifference, leaving her to cope with her father's scorn resting squarely and solely on her slender shoulders.

Unconsciously she stiffened those shoulders as she removed the nozzle from the rental car's tank and replaced it on the petrol bowser.

"So it is you."

The low pitch of his voice had matured; it was deeper, richer, than it had been ten years ago. The sound of it still had the power to send a shiver down her spine, a shiver quite different to the old days. But then, she had to expect that, didn't she? Neither of them were still the same.

He lifted a tanned hand to slide expensive sunglasses down the aristocratic bridge of his nose. She wished he hadn't done that. She would have preferred the barrier, however tiny, between her gaze and the stormy look that crossed his as their eyes met. Fine lines feathered from the corners of his eyes as they adjusted to the sudden glare of bright February summer sunlight reflected off the concrete forecourt. Eyes the colour of liquid amber. Eyes that held her, for a split second, trapped in the past, immobilised, rendered speechless.

Lily swallowed convulsively, desperate to relieve the arid dryness in her throat. She felt the precise second his attention swept from her face to the muscles working in her neck. Tiny flickers of heat grew where his gaze touched. Damn him for still having that effect on her.

"You're not what I expected." Jack didn't so much as blink.

"What were you expecting?" Lily lifted her chin and met his stare full-on.

Instantly she knew her mistake. You never beard a lion in its own den. She should have ignored him, gone in and paid for her petrol and left.

"Certainly not someone who could pump her own gas," he drawled, snapping her out of her temporary fugue.

Goaded, she couldn't hold back her reply. "It's amazing what can happen when someone grows up then, isn't it? I can't say you're what I was expecting, either." She flicked what she hoped was a scathing gaze over the fine tailored suit he wore right down to the hand-tooled Italian leather shoes that encased his feet. Yes, she noticed things like that. It was what had kept her afloat in the artificial world she'd dwelled in for far too long. "Not exactly a part-time fuel-pump boy anymore. Still remember how to do it?"

His eyes narrowed speculatively at her careless remark. Lily gave an inward groan. When would she learn to shut up and let silence be her voice?

"You know what I meant, Jack." She spun away from him, her Manolos clicking a staccato echo in her wake.

His eyes continued to bore a virtual hole into her back as she went inside the store and paid for her gas. She could feel it, like the searing concentration of power from a magnifying glass in the sun. It was a relief to get inside the petrol station store, to hear the tinted sliding doors whoosh shut behind her.

She didn't know what she had expected inside but it certainly wasn't the modernised countertop and the stands of groceries and household consumables that stood in colourful rows. Time hadn't stood still here. She wasn't the only one who had changed since her ignominious departure from a town she'd learned to loathe with every cell in her body.

The swish of the automatic opening doors behind her and that same tantalising waft of sandalwood and lime gave her advance warning of Jack's approach. With a swift smile she accepted her receipt from the attendant and turned to leave only to find her way barred by six-foot-plus of solid never-take-no-for-an-answer male.

"What brings you back, Lily?" His tone was couched in a way that wouldn't alert any eavesdropping ears to the history that hung between them, but there was no mistaking the seriousness in his eyes.

"Nothing in particular," she lied as smoothly as she could. She wasn't about to unload her financial woes on Jack's shoulders any time this millennium. "Just thought it was time for a trip back."

"So you won't be here long then?" His eyes became blank, making it harder to read what was behind his question.

"Long enough, Jack. I don't have any plans to leave in a hurry. Satisfied?"

"Leaving in a hurry was your speciality, wasn't it? And as to whether I'm satisfied…" He let his voice trail away.

Heat bloomed across Lily's chest and up her neck. She grabbed her sunglasses out of her handbag, shoved them onto her face and stalked out to her waiting car—

her brief sanctuary. She was shaking as she opened her car door and settled into the seat. She had the engine running and the car in gear when a loud knock on her driver's window made her jump.

Jack. What now? She stifled her irritation and the scathing remark begging to be freed from her tongue and instead flipped the switch that lowered the car window.

"Yes?" She imbued the monosyllabic question with as much tedium as she could manage.

Her heart lurched as Jack's face softened into a smile. Even after all these years he could still see straight through her and quite clearly knew how much his comment had rattled her.

"It's been a long time," he drawled. "Let's not get off on the wrong foot. I apologise for baiting you back there. I didn't mean to upset you on your first trip home."

"Yeah, whatever, Jack. No offence taken. Water under the bridge and all that."

He didn't take his hand off the windowsill and Lily's foot itched to press down on the accelerator and just get away. She stared pointedly at his fingers—trying, and failing, to indicate he should remove them from her vehicle. His hands were broad, his fingers long and neatly manicured. Somewhat different and vastly more polished than those of the apprentice motor mechanic who had caressed her teenage body to giddy heights so long ago. A sudden pull of longing from deep inside her womb made her fight to suppress a gasp.

Coming home had been a terrible mistake.

"I'll see you around." The way he said it made it a certainty, not just an observation.

"Yeah. Later, then."

Her knuckles were white where she gripped the steering wheel and she forced herself to relax, breathing from deep in her diaphragm. He took his hand off the sill and gave her a small wave. Lily put her car into gear and eased away from the forecourt. She doubted she'd be seeing Jack Dolan anytime soon. Not if she had any choice in the matter. The water that had flowed under their particular bridge had been turbulent and full of debris, enough to undermine their supports and bring the bridge crashing down.

Well, there was one thing in favour of having met up with him so early on in her return to Onemata. It was over and done with. Now all she had to do was to face her father—oh, and get her life together. Her mouth twisted into a rueful smile, if only it was that simple.

As she drove through the town at the base of the peninsula she noticed the changes—some subtle, some not. It was both familiar and strange at the same time, and left her unsettled. No less so because of the direction she was taking toward her father's beachfront home near the distant tip of the finger of land that gave Onemata its name. She hadn't set foot inside the house since the night he'd ripped her teen romance with Jack into tiny pieces and ordered her away to Auckland. Since then, unwilling to return, she'd stayed in New Zealand's largest city for a couple of years, attending university and enjoying the anonymity of being one of many instead of being in the town where everyone knew each other's business.

A chance encounter with a modelling scout had seen

her catapulted into *Fashion Week* and then overseas. Returning to Onemata had been the furthest thing from her mind. But there came a time in everyone's life when they had to take stock and assess their direction. A succession of poor investments, on top of a persistent bout of mono that made it impossible for her to accept new work, made that time now.

Jack watched through narrowed eyes as Lily drove away from him and through the main street of town. Did she even know that most of it was his? he wondered. Did she have any idea of what she was dealing with now she was home?

He doubted it.

His body still radiated the heat that had flamed through him at the first sight of her. He'd thought he'd have been immune after all these years, but no. His reaction had been as instantaneous and immediate as the first day she'd turned up at Onemata High. Hot, hard and hungry for a taste of her.

She was thinner than she used to be, almost fragile-looking, and there was a distance in her pale blue eyes he'd never encountered in her before. A distance that reminded him of her father and his business ethics.

Jack's vow, the one that had driven him to the peak of Australasia's business elite, echoed through his mind. The Fontaine family would never again wreak harm on those dear to him.

His mind ticked over, weighing his next move. Lily's arrival home was more portentous, and less of her own making, than she realised. Over the past few years he'd systematically bought out every asset previously owned by Charles Fontaine, and was now poised for the coup de grâce—the decimation of Fontaine Compuware, Charles Fontaine's own mother lode of wealth, within the next month. How rich would be the satisfaction to use Lily Fontaine as a tactical weapon in his final campaign? Oh yeah, Charles had it coming to him, all right. And so did his deceitful daughter.

Lily knew she should be back up in the house having something to eat and gearing up to face her father when he returned home from the office. Instead she hunched in the sand dunes, oblivious to the lights spilling behind her and across the manicured lawn from the two-storied Spanish-style house her father had built as a monument to his wealth, her eyes fixed on the glittering beauty of moonlight reflected on the heaving sea and foaming water. Tonight, each hungry, rolling wave appeared to relentlessly devour another piece of the shoreline as it advanced and retreated with military precision.

Onemata had that effect on you, she decided. Bit by bit, it consumed. Slowly. Inexorably.

There'd been a brief handwritten note from the housekeeper, Mrs. Manson, waiting for her when she'd let herself in with her old key. Her father had been detained at the office and she was to make herself at home and not to wait dinner for him.

A wave of guilt had swept through her at the relief she'd felt when she knew she had a brief respite from their reunion. Guilt followed by a pang of hurt that he couldn't be bothered to be home when she'd arrived.

The distance that the years away had given her was nothing. It had passed in a blink. She'd sworn she'd never come back, a tearful promise made into her sodden pillow after her father had sent her to Auckland. To anyone who'd asked, she'd gone up to start university there, but there'd been more to it. Her father had seen. He'd known. And the knowledge had shamed him. *She* had shamed him.

While her father had driven her to leave, Jack Dolan had made certain she'd never want to return. In those first few weeks after she'd gone she'd hoped with all her heart he'd return her phone call, that he'd find some way to come after her. But he hadn't so much as tried to contact her. Not once. He'd chosen to accept her father's money rather than her love. His rejection had been more painful than she'd ever believed possible, and she knew all about pain.

Now here she was. Home. For most people the four-letter word invoked warmth and comfort. The secure knowledge that whatever you'd done, wherever you'd been and whoever you'd become, you could always come back to a sense of family and belonging. But not for her, not now.

Try as she might over the years of self-exile, she still couldn't come to terms with how her father had treated her like nothing more than a business enterprise. Throwing money at her whenever a problem arose. Knowing his wealth would keep her occupied like a child at an amusement park. While she was certain he'd dined out on her success as a model and society hostess, emotionally he'd all but washed his hands of her.

Charles Fontaine had been the strength and backbone of her childhood, of everything she'd known and believed in. Yes, he'd been a hard man, unyielding and intractable at times, but since her parents' divorce when she was four he'd always been there—unlike her mother who'd thrown herself into a new life with a new family and who'd cut off all ties with her daughter without a backward glance. Her father had always been her rock. Until she'd hit her teens and began to question his edicts. Until she'd started going out with Jack. Her father's bluster and rage had made it easy to transfer her reliance onto Jack, had even made it part of the thrill of seeing her forbidden lover, but even Jack had let her down in the end.

Unconsciously she fisted a handful of sand. The hurt still lived there, buried deep inside. They'd been so young. Too young to be in love? To young to plan a future? She hadn't thought so at the time.

Lily dragged the brakes on her wayward thoughts and expelled a harsh breath. Wasting time on the past achieved nothing. She knew that fact as intimately as she knew her face in the mirror.

Her fingers relaxed and she allowed the cold, gritty particles to trickle away. Despite the damp night air, Lily couldn't drag herself away from the beach. She'd been drawn here tonight, to this one place that still held some happy memories. Snatches of laughter, warmth and a naive belief that love conquered all forced their way past the walls she'd erected to confine her memories. For the briefest moment she allowed herself to remember without pain, before firmly pushing them back where they belonged.

Clouds scudded across the sky, obscuring the silver radiance of the moon and cloaking the beach in darkness. It was time to go back in. Time to face reality.

Back inside the house Lily made straight for the bathroom and peeled off her clothing. Without so much as a glance at herself in the mirror she reached into the shower stall and turned the mixer to as hot as she could bear before stepping inside. She leaned her arms against the shower wall and let the soothing heat of the water cascade over the back of her head, neck and shoulders.

She squeezed her eyes shut and tipped back her head so the spray hit her full-force in the face. Lord, but she was tired. Since she'd received news from her accountant of the failed venture capital investment, sleep had been ephemeral. The deal had seemed so secure. She'd invested most of her savings—a sound move, she'd believed, and one that had supposedly guaranteed a solid return. Income she'd been counting on since illness had forced her out of the limelight, off the A-list and into virtual unemployment. In her subsequent bid to reclaim her life and be seen in the right places, she'd forged for herself a whole new image. Unfortunately the party-girl image was at odds with the elegant and stylish look her fashion house preferred and her contract hadn't been renewed. Coming home to daddy had been her last resort.

Blindly, Lily reached for the shower gel and began to lather her body, briefly luxuriating in the sensation of the foaming liquid against her skin. Her hands lingered over her softly curved belly and her hips, where a barely visible tracery of fine silver lines striated the skin. The pain of loss expanded, sharp and fast, hitching her breath and driving a moan from her lips. Every now and then it hit her like that—the memory, the loss of her stillborn baby boy and most of all of Jack's rejection of them both.

Two

Lily squeezed her eyes tight against the tears that swelled in her eyes. She had to pull it together—just like she'd learned to do so many times before. All that the world would see would be Lily Fontaine, ex-model and former companion to the rich and famous.

Lily turned off the water and reached for her towel. She quickly dried herself and wrapped the towel around her. A massive yawn split her face. She hadn't slept during the flight from Los Angeles, and jet lag was catching up. Her father still wasn't home. It looked as if he was in as much of a hurry to welcome his only child back as she'd been in to get here.

A loud knock at the front door made her jump. Lily dropped her towel to pull a flimsy rose-pink satin robe from the top of her open suitcase and tied it around her as she trotted down the stairs to the front entrance. A glance at the grandfather clock guarding the tiled area confirmed it was getting late. She hoped whoever was at the door wasn't in a talkative mood. With a smile pasted firmly on her face, Lily flung open the front door.

"Oh, it's you."

Her smile died an instant death as Jack filled the door frame. Dressed only in her robe, she suddenly felt painfully vulnerable. Lily grabbed the lapels closer together.

"What do you want?" She pitched her voice to be as cool and unwelcoming as the night air that swirled around her bare legs.

"You'll freeze like that." Jack stepped through the doorway, forcing Lily to back up rapidly.

She'd felt at a disadvantage before, at the petrol station, but this was much worse. Jack loomed over her, tall and dark. His crisp white shirt, accented with a silk tie the colour of spun gold, and charcoal suit emphasised his even tan. He always had tanned well, and exploring how far that rich caramel colour extended had kept her enticed for hours. She clutched the edges of the robe tight to try to rid herself of the sensation. The memory of the texture of his skin left an intangible tingle in its wake.

Jack turned and shut the front door behind him. In that instant the entrance, which had always felt so airy and spacious, closed in.

"Aren't you going to invite me in?"

Lily huffed in frustration. Obviously he wasn't planning on making this a short visit.

"Look, Jack, can we take a rain check on whatever it is you have to say? My flight in from L.A. was delayed, and the drive down from Auckland has left me absolutely whacked. I'm struggling to keep my eyes open."

He lifted a finger to gently stroke the hollow underneath one eye. Lily forced herself to stay still, not to flinch back in shock at the tenderness of his touch, or the sudden flare of his pupils.

"I won't keep you long."

Ignoring her gasp, he walked through the foyer and toward the back of the house, to the kitchen and family room situated away from the formal rooms on this floor. With no other option, she followed him down the hall.

Lily hadn't been in the newly refurbished family room yet. Her father had spoken to her on the phone about what he'd done, knocking out a couple of walls to create a more casual lounge for him to use when he wasn't entertaining for business. As usual the room was a picture of perfection—almost as if it had come straight from the pages of a home and lifestyle magazine. A cluster of photographs sat on a table to one side, mostly studio shots of her, she noted, and roomy couches faced one another in front of a creamy-white Hinuera-stone-framed gas fireplace. Whatever his reasons for creating such an elegant room, he certainly didn't spend any time in here. The couches were pristine, not so much as a dented cushion to show where anyone had sat, and the coffee table coasters were stacked in their holder as if redundant.

Taking a wide berth around Jack she went into the kitchen, letting her fingertips trail on the cool black-granite countertops before she filled the jug with water and set it to boil.

"Since you're here, d'you want a coffee?" she asked

as she retrieved mugs from the cupboard and a jar of freeze-dried coffee from the pantry.

"Sure. No milk, thanks."

So he hadn't changed that much, she thought as she went through the motions. For all that Jack had bowled his way in here tonight, he didn't seem to be in much of a hurry to talk. The jug seemed to take an inordinate amount of time to come to the boil and she fidgeted uncomfortably.

Across the room Jack lifted a hand to gently finger the fronds of a bird's nest fern in a colourful ceramic pot on the wooden casual dining table. Her body tightened. His hands, his fingers, his lips, his mouth. He'd always been gentle. But that wasn't who he was now, she reminded herself sternly. There was no softness in the man who stood before her.

"So, what did you want, Jack?" Her sharp query echoed in the quiet room.

He turned his head to face her, a faint curl to his lips, and for the briefest moment she saw the heated spark in his golden eyes before it was ruthlessly snuffed out. He casually flicked open the buttons on his jacket, letting the fabric swing away to expose the breadth of his chest rising and falling beneath the fine, crisp, cotton of his shirt. Unbidden, visions flooded her mind—of her fingers tangled in the sprinkling of darkly curled hair on his chest. Her lips pressed against him. The warm taste of his skin against her tongue.

Her breath caught and her mouth dried before she regained a tenuous grip on her control. It was the jet lag. It had to be the jet lag. It'd been far too long for him to still have this mesmerising power over her. She had spent most of the past ten years working hard to forget him. She was a woman of the world. Well-versed in the intricacies of social interaction. Allowing herself to be turned on, like a cheap light bulb, because of a few memories was not on the cards.

Her eyes riveted on his implacable face as he started to walk toward her. She took a step back on legs that had begun to tremble. He stopped within inches of her, but she was determined to stand her ground this time. Heat emanated from his body, bringing with it the scent of his aftershave. The spice and tangy citrus fragrance tantalised and teased at her nostrils. Lily drew in a shuddering breath. Jack slowly raised his hand.

Oh no, please no. Don't touch me again. Her heart rate accelerated, suffusing her body with heat. As much as she dreaded the sensation of his touch she felt herself lean forward ever so slightly.

His hand hesitated then dropped back to his side.

"What's your thing these days, Lily?" His voice was deep, enquiring. "Still toying with a trip on the wild side?"

She stiffened her spine in reaction to his words. There was no way on this earth she'd let him know how much his barb stung. While they'd been going out together all her friends had teased her about Jack's family being from the "wrong side" of town, and how going out with him in the face of her father's distinct disapproval was taking a trip on the "wild side." Lily shook her head slightly, her tone surprisingly level when she spoke.

"You don't know me anymore. Times change."

"Sure, time does, but people don't. Not really, not deep inside."

He expelled a sigh of disgust and she felt his breath, warm and moist, against her throat. Her pulse throbbed in a crazy tattoo.

"Look, forget the coffee. Just say what you came to say, then go." Her voice was but a whisper, a plea.

Jack regretted the move to stand so close to Lily the moment he came to a halt in front of her, but the scent of her—freshly washed and still dewy-damp—filled his nostrils and kept him captive where he was. He fisted his hands to stop himself from reaching for her again—his instinctive touch to her face when he arrived, an action he already regretted deeply. An indistinct growl murmured from his throat. Lily's lips parted on a breath and his senses clouded with the almost irresistible urge to drop his lips to hers. To taste her again. To see if she still responded like a flame on dry kindling. To sink against her soft mouth, to lose himself in it and find…what?

Heat rose within him as he dropped his gaze from her lips to where her robe had parted slightly, tiny creases marred the fabric where she'd gripped it with those slender, elegant hands. Hands that had never done an honest day's work in her life. A stray droplet of water from her wet hair trickled across her collarbone before dipping into the shadowed valley of softly rounded flesh—flesh that barely moved, as if she were holding her breath. Waiting for his next move.

His groin tightened as he watched her nipples constrict into tight twin buds that pressed against the satin fabric of her robe. A gentle flush of warm colour suffused her chest and spread up her neck. Arousal. Jack's mouth dried as the rest of his body answered the call of hers. Slowly, he bent his head.

What the hell was he doing? Icy reality sluiced through him and he stepped away. Lily staggered slightly as if her balance had shifted, and he shot out his hands to steady her. The brief contact burned like a brand across his palms. Bad move, he told himself as his hands brushed heated skin through sensuously slippery material. A sharp jolt of desire jarred his body.

Very bad move.

Where was that famous boardroom cool now? It was as if the teenage hormones that had drawn him to Lily in the first place still drove him—and he didn't like it one bit. With slow deliberation he removed his hands, shoved them deeply into his pockets, and took a few steps back.

Lily knew the instant he had himself under control. If was as if a shutter had crashed down, hiding the unleashed passion that had flared in his leonine eyes and left a cold shell in its place. She should hate him for that—the remote and indifferent expression, so at odds with the Jack Dolan of her youth. The Jack Dolan who had let her down in the worst kind of way, she reminded herself bitterly. But even so, her lips still throbbed in anticipation, her entire body hummed with expectancy.

Breathe, she told herself, and inhaled a deep breath before letting it out slowly. Tiny tremors rocked her body. Temptation and torture. It had always been the same with him.

They'd been worlds apart—she, the indulged daughter of the richest man in town. Jack, the son of one of her father's employees and a tearaway from the wrong side of the tracks. When she'd started at the local high school, after she'd begged her father to be freed from the boarding school she'd suffered at for two miserable years, Jack had been a senior. Their attraction, their connection, had been instant and intense—and she'd been innocent enough to think they could overcome the differences in their lives. They'd had the same dreams for success, the same goals to reach together—until the night she'd been forced to leave without him and he'd chosen not to follow.

As tired as she was, there was nothing Lily wanted to do more right now than to climb into her rental car and drive back to the airport and hop on the first plane out of New Zealand. But she'd made a promise to herself. No more running away.

"I've planned a barbecue tomorrow night. I thought you might like to come along. Reacquaint yourself with some of the old gang."

Jack's invitation was the last thing she expected. Sounded like it was bound to be bags of fun—not.

"Look, I've only just arrived back..." she started to say.

"And here I thought you were the queen of the social circuit. Scared, Lily?"

"Of course not. I don't even know what Dad has organised for me. I can't say for sure if I can come." The words blustered past her lips. Lord, she sounded like a total fool.

"Ah, yes. Your father. How was the family reunion?"

"Fine," Lily replied through gritted teeth. There was no way she was letting Jack know her father hadn't so much as called to welcome her home yet. "Give me your details and if I can make it, I will. Okay?"

Jack gave her a narrow-eyed stare before slipping a business card holder and a pen from his breast pocket and flicking out a card. His pen strokes were swift slashes across the small white rectangle. He held it out to her.

"Seven o'clock, Lily. I'll look forward to seeing you there. Dress casual, hmm? There won't be any paparazzi to distract you."

The scathing look on his face as he made reference to the photographers and journalists who'd highlighted her rise to fame and her slide back down again told her quite clearly what he thought. But he also told her far more than he probably realised. He might not have followed her that night, but he'd followed her career since. Somehow, the knowledge didn't give her the satisfaction she thought it would.

Three

Lily woke with the grogginess that comes from having slept the deep sleep of utter exhaustion. Her father had arrived home shortly after Jack's departure and he'd been brusque at best. Distracted, he'd given her a perfunctory kiss on the cheek and suggested they talk in the morning. She tried to convince herself it was no more than she'd expected, but a small part of her felt like the little girl at a school recital futilely waiting for her daddy to turn up to watch her dance.

Lily stretched out on the cotton sheets of her bed and listened to the nearby crash of waves on the shore and the cries of seagulls as they swooped across the sand. The beach called to her, as it had every morning before she'd been sent away. Lily quickly freshened up then dragged sweatpants and a T-shirt from her suitcase on the floor and scrabbled deeper in the mess of luggage for her running shoes. She should think about unpacking when she got back from her run but somehow the idea of putting her clothes away implied a level of permanence she wasn't ready for—not yet.

As she ran lightly down the stairs she realised how silent the house was. It was unusual for her father to still be asleep at this time of the day, weekday or not. A brief note left on the kitchen bench informed her he'd had to go into work early but invited her to drive out to meet him at his office for lunch.

Lily scrunched the note into a tight ball in her hand and let it drop onto the countertop. After all this time he still hadn't forgiven her. That much was patently clear.

Stifling her disappointment, Lily let herself out the sliding-glass door and onto the patio that led to stairs that took her down onto the beach. Within seconds she was stretching out her legs in a leisurely lope along the hard-packed sand. The sun was only just beginning to dispel the grey gloom of dawn. A trickle of something filtered through her mind—of rightness, of belonging. Lily shook her thoughts free before they could take a firmer hold. At this stage she wasn't certain she could stay here for the long term. But then again, what choice did she have?

Lily forced her legs to work harder, faster, and she ate up the distance along the sand. She was determined to regain her fitness one way or the other, but breathlessness forced her to slow slightly as she neared the end of the strand of shoreline. There were more houses along the beachfront than there had been when she left

Onemata, holiday homes for the most part, by the look of them. That kind of progress was only to be expected, but she couldn't help but feel a pang of loss for the encroachment of civilisation on her childhood playground. She slowed to a stop as she drew level with a huge new house facing the beach. It certainly had a presence many of the holiday homes lacked.

Nestled in the curve of the bay where the towering cliff side tapered down to the beach, the house looked solid and permanent. Massive retaining poles supported a wide deck that was bound to give spectacular views out over the sea and up the sweeping line of the beach toward the point. Twin staircases at either end of the deck burrowed down to the beach and full-length, one-way-mirror-glass windows faced the entire frontage of the building. A large balcony off the top floor provided a deep porch underneath—a haven, no doubt, from the hot summer sun. While essentially modern in design, the house still held an aura of Colonial influence, an echo of the older buildings in town that harked back a hundred years or more. It was in total contrast to the Mediterranean-style whitewashed villa her father had erected many years ago, and seemed to fit the landscape as if it had been here for years.

A solitary figure stood at the edge of the deck railing, his forearms resting on the top rail and his all too familiar face turned to the rising sun. Lily's stomach sank. It figured it would be Jack. She did a wide turn and faced back the other way down the beach, back to where she'd come from. The irony of that symbolism wasn't lost on her. Back to where she'd come from. Ha! The short bitter laugh held no humour for her at all.

"Lily!"

She increased her pace. She could pretend she hadn't heard the strong male shout that coasted on the wind.

Her chest was getting tight. She'd pushed herself too hard this morning. It'd been far too long since she'd stretched her physical limits like this and the doctor had warned her not to expect too much too soon. The muscles in her thighs and calves began to burn, a stitch started in her side.

The steady pounding of heavier feet caught up behind her and Lily tried with all she had to push herself the final short distance to the stairs that led to her father's property.

"Hold up before you kill yourself."

Strong hands caught at her shoulders, forcing her to draw to a close. He must have sprinted the distance between them; she thought as her breath came in ragged spurts and, curse him, he hadn't even raised a sweat.

"Why—why did you stop me?" She bent at the waist, dragged in one heaving breath after another.

"Just being neighbourly."

His short dark hair was tousled by his run, a few strands slipping across his broad forehead. Her fingers itched to smooth them back but she maintained her grip on her trembling thighs.

"Neighbourly?" She barked out a short laugh. "Yeah, right."

"Are you coming tonight?" he asked, direct and to the point.

"I told you, I need to see if Dad has any plans for me."

Jack just looked at her. Was that pity in his eyes? She couldn't bear it. Not from him.

She straightened and met his gaze. "Look, I'll probably be there. He's tied up a lot with work by the looks of things, so yeah. I'll be there."

A glimmer of a smile played around his lips and, despite herself, Lily found herself answering in kind.

"Seven o'clock, remember."

"Fine." Lily turned and started up the stairs to the house. "Is there anything you'd like me to bring?"

"Just yourself. I believe I can provide everything else."

"My, how times have changed." Lily couldn't stop the words from tumbling from her mouth.

Jack's jaw firmed and his lips pressed tight together before he answered. "Don't be more of a bitch than you can help, Lily. It won't win you any new friends."

"And the old ones?" she asked without hesitation. What about them? Had they shucked her off as easily as Jack had? It wasn't as if she'd made any particularly close female friends. Coming as she had from boarding school, she'd been an outsider from the start of her time at Onemata High. The only person she'd been close to had been Jack; he hadn't left any room for anyone else.

"Most of them were coming anyway, but there'll be a few who'll come just to check you out."

"Gee, I can't wait." Lily already regretted accepting his invitation. "See you at seven, then."

"I'm looking forward to it." His answering drawl sent a shiver of apprehension down her spine.

"Sure you are," she muttered under her breath as she continued up the short staircase that led to her father's property. It wasn't until she'd slid the ranch slider closed with a solid thud that he finally started back down the beach.

Lily dressed up for the meeting with her father. He'd expect it and it gave her confidence a boost to put on one of the designer outfits she'd squeezed into her suitcases in her rush from Los Angeles. Once she'd made her decision to come home she had fast-tracked everything she could to get there. It wasn't as if there was anything still holding her there. As her profile had waned so too had the friendliness of the clique she moved around in. It had been time for a clean break.

The offices at FonCom, as Fontaine Compuware was locally known, had been refurbished since the last time she'd been there. Obviously no expense had been spared. Business must be good, she observed.

"Lily!" Her father's voice boomed down the corridor as he came into reception to meet her.

In a whirl of activity he showed her around his staff and the offices. She felt as if she was on show and she smiled until her cheeks ached. Obviously the news of her ignominious fall from grace with her fashion house had been as widely touted here at home. But her father, in his usual fashion, was set to steamroller over everyone's preconceptions about her.

It was a relief when Charles Fontaine settled her opposite him at the seafood restaurant near his offices, away from the overeager gazes and the prying questions.

He looked more tired than she remembered. Last night she'd put it down to having worked late, but in the crisp light of day he looked worn out, the colour in his cheeks unnaturally high.

They gave their orders and settled back in their seats, each eyeing the other.

"Mrs. Manson tells me she saw you with Jack Dolan this morning." Charles Fontaine came straight to the point.

"Are you spying on me, Dad?" *Already?*

"Is it true?"

Lily sighed in exasperation. "Yes, it's true. What of it? I am twenty-eight years old and perfectly capable of looking after myself."

"Pshaw!" His snort left her in no doubt he thought nothing of the kind. "Did you arrange to meet him?"

"No, of course I didn't. I went for a run on the beach. I had no idea he had a property there. He saw me and followed me home."

"Chased you like a dog, from what I heard."

Lily stiffened. "And so what if he did?"

"I thought you'd learned your lesson from that guy. Best you stay away from him, Lily, my girl."

"I make my own decisions about who I see and who I don't see." Lily felt as if she was a teenager once again, being hauled over the coals for having been seen in the company of "that Dolan boy" after school. When would her father learn he couldn't meddle in other people's lives?

"Just thought I'd say my piece. I don't want to see you hurt again. Not like before." Charles looked up to the waiter who'd brought their meals and bestowed one of his rare smiles. "Thank you, Johnno. That'll be all."

Lily bit back her retort. It would be a waste of energy

anyway. She looked across the table at the massive platter of deep-fried seafood and fries on her father's plate.

"Dad, are you looking after yourself okay? Are you certain you should be eating all that?"

"Never you mind, my girl. Let me be the judge of what's best for me." He picked up a fork and speared a French fry before dipping it in the side dish of tartare sauce and then into the tomato sauce dish, as well, before popping it into his mouth. He munched away with an expression on his face that came closer to joy than he'd had when he laid eyes on her last night. "Now, where were we? Ah, yes, that Dolan boy. You'll stay away from him, won't you?"

Hadn't he listened to a word she'd said? Obviously not. Well, it was time he had a wakeup call.

"I didn't say anything of the kind, Dad. You said it." Tension coiled in her stomach. Home less than one day and already they were set to be at loggerheads.

"That's right, my girl. I said it. Just you remember that and we'll get along fine. Now, aside from *him,* have you caught up with any of your friends yet?"

Lily hesitated before answering. "Not yet, although I've been invited to a barbecue to catch up with a few of them tonight." It wasn't exactly a lie.

"Good, good. I'm glad you're going to be occupied. Have to work late again. No rest for the wicked. Ha!"

His laugh at his own joke sounded forced even to Lily's ears. There was something obviously pressing on him, but theirs wasn't the kind of relationship where she could ask him what was wrong. Instead Lily applied herself to her calamari and salad and decided quietly to herself to have a word with Mrs. Manson about the type of food her father ate at home. If she had no other influence on his life, Lily would make sure he ate more healthily than now.

Her father steered their conversation along more general lines for the rest of their lunch, talking loudly about her work and turning heads in a way that made Lily want to crawl under the tablecloth and hide. Instead, she sat with perfect posture and a plastic smile on her face and counted the minutes until he blessedly went back to the office.

Four

Lily's car rolled to a stop on the crushed-shell driveway. She cut the engine and pulled her keys from the ignition. Seven twenty-five. She was running late. From the number of cars already parked in the large parking bay, very late. No doubt it would give Jack another reason to take a swipe at her. If her father hadn't been so adamant about her not seeing anything of Jack she probably would have called with her apologies by now. In fact, torn between going and another night at home alone, she'd prevaricated for the better part of an hour about whether to come, then another hour about what to wear.

A gust of wind whipped around the side of the house and pulled wisps of hair from the pins she'd eventually struggled with in her decision to give everyone what they expected. Lily Fontaine, fashion model and socialite.

He said "dress casual." So she did. For her. Her strategically torn jeans exposed a glimpse of tanned thighs. The low-slung waist brought attention to the bejewelled belly bar in her navel, while her impossibly high and dainty sandals and silky golden halter top screamed catwalk chic in foot-high letters. Her clothing was her armour and something told her she'd need every link of it tonight. She climbed out of the car and stiffened her spine as she walked toward the sweeping staircase leading to Jack's front door. This side of the house was no less imposing than the beach frontage; the landscaping around the driveway and parking bay leading to the entrance enhanced the obvious wealth it had taken to create such an architectural dream.

Her heels echoed on the wooden stairs, heels she'd chosen for the advantage of the added height they'd bring to her five-foot-ten. Wearing these she'd almost be eye level with Jack—on a par. The front door swung open as she approached, just as another wickedly intentioned gust of wind plucked at her hair, loosening another strand to fall softly about her face.

Jack stood in the doorway. A sudden hunger painted stark on his features as she approached. His unblinking, burning scrutiny sent a cold bead of fear straight to her heart. Maybe she'd gone too far with her choice of clothing tonight. It didn't take a rocket scientist to figure out she wasn't wearing a bra under the sensuously soft fabric of her top, and the dropped cowl neck swayed enough with her graceful movements to reveal the swell of her breasts with each step.

"You're late." His words were clipped.

"Yeah, sorry about that." She wouldn't give him the satisfaction of an excuse. That would imply she cared about his opinion—and she didn't, not anymore.

"Are you, Lily?"

"Am I what?"

"Sorry."

She dipped her head, refusing to make eye contact or to acknowledge his question again.

"Come through." He gestured her through the entrance and down a short passage that opened out into a spacious open-plan living area.

Lounge furniture was arranged in front of the windows in a way that offered every guest a view of the ocean. To the right a formal dining suite sat under a modern iron candelabra-style light fitting. Several people stood in small groups, both indoors and out on the deck. Their silhouettes lit by the sun, low in the sky and casting its gilding light across the calm ocean. A few people turned and stared at her before turning back to their group. Lily's stomach clenched with nerves.

"This is nice," she said, looking around the room and noticing the artwork on the walls.

"Its home," Jack answered noncommittally.

He was right. It was a home. Lily's experienced eye could just about put a price on every item there and while everything was perfect and in its place there was a genuine warmth about the room and the furnishings that made you feel as if you could flop down on one of the wide leather sofas in front of the cheery glass-fronted wood-burning stove, slip off your shoes and tuck your legs under you in absolute comfort.

"You live here on your own?" Darn it, why did she ask that? It's not as if she cared.

"For now."

Well, wasn't he the master of brief conversation tonight, she thought with irritation. That was going to make things awkward. She'd only just arrived and already she felt like she'd done three rounds in an emotional boxing ring.

She allowed herself to be soothed by the soft song of an Italian tenor played discreetly in the background, the rich timbre of the soloist's voice weaving around her senses. Jack lifted a bottle of champagne from the ice bucket on the table and filled a slender crystal flute with an experienced hand.

"Champagne?" he asked.

"Thank you."

Lily assiduously avoided touching his fingers as he passed her the glass filled with the foaming golden liquid.

Jack watched as she took a sip of the wine, a little of the moisture leaving a glistening imprint on her lips. A small tremor shook her hand. She was nervous. Good. The movement of lifting her arm caused the gossamer-fine material of her top to shift again—movement he'd been aware of from the second he'd opened the front door to his house. From where he stood, to the side, he could almost see the lower curve of her breast.

Had that heart-shaped birthmark on the underside of her left breast faded at all in the past ten years? he wondered. Or was it still there, begging to be traced with his tongue? A surge of need coursed through him, sending a flood of desire to pool in his groin. Seducing her would certainly be no hardship. Convincing her, now there would be the challenge, and there was nothing in life that Jack loved more than a challenge.

He put a hand to her elbow and guided her through the bifold doors that led out onto the spacious deck. "Come and meet everyone. They're looking forward to seeing you again."

"I'll just bet they are."

Was that fear in her voice or just the cynicism she appeared to wear like a cloak around her slender shoulders these days? Probably more likely the former. Jack knew he should feel some sense of compassion for her but it was a commodity he was very short on when it came to the Fontaines. Charles Fontaine had destroyed his father, ruined his whole family, without a second thought. The man, and his daughter, would pay dearly.

He slid his arm around her lower back and guided her from one group to the other, the consummate host, and introduced her to the people she didn't already know—reacquainting her with their old friends. Surprisingly it all went extremely well and she slotted into conversation with everyone with a minimum of awkwardness. There was the occasional slanted remark but Lily brushed them all off with a smile and a joke. Jack could begin to see why she'd been so popular in the party circuit overseas. She had a way with people that made them feel comfortable and made them laugh. But something about her laughter, the way she spoke, made him feel like she was putting on an act.

It was soon apparent that everyone there was treating them like a couple and it served his purpose to continue to nurture that misconception. Wherever Lily went, he was never far from her, until eventually she stayed at his side by choice. The simplicity with which it had happened suited him on many levels. Not least of which was that it was the most effective way to dim the avaricious gleam in the eyes of the single, and even some of the married, men there. If his plan was to succeed he'd have to make certain that Lily didn't hook up with anyone else.

Much later in the night, and long after the last of the dinner leftovers and dishes had been cleared away, those who hadn't had to dash home to relieve babysitters congregated down on the beach to toast marshmallows over a driftwood fire. Conversation lowered to gentle murmurs. One of the guys had brought his guitar and sat quietly strumming. If they could have turned back the clock ten years it couldn't have been more idyllic. Except there was no way to turn back time and make things right. The only way to make things right was to take effective action, and that was something Jack excelled at.

"So what brings you back to Onemata, Lily?" a voice called through the flickering flames as they licked their way over the twisted logs.

Jack felt her stiffen at his side. What would she say? he wondered. Would she admit to being virtually broke? Being forced by necessity to come home with her tail between those enticingly long and slender legs of hers. Living, as she had, so prominently in the public eye hadn't left much to the imagination. And as for any secrets? Well, it was amazing what people would disclose when given the right financial incentive. Yes, he knew her secrets. All of them. No general strategised a battle without sufficient intelligence beforehand. It had cost a small fortune but he was determined to keep the upper hand. He wouldn't be the loser this time.

"I'd been unwell. I needed a break and, let's face it, who wouldn't come here to recuperate," she answered with a small laugh.

"Nothing too serious I hope," Jack said softly, turning his head slightly to speak to her and her alone. He knew exactly how serious it had been. Not life-threatening, but certainly enough to disrupt her career and to see her agent release her from their contract. She herself had managed to do the rest of the damage by hanging about with the wrong set, being seen in the right places but doing the wrong headline-seeking things. Her subsequent exposure had had the desired effect from Jack's point of view. It had seen to the commencement of her fall from grace. It couldn't have worked better if he'd planned it himself, and it had crossed his mind to do so. In the end, it had all come down to Lily. And she'd delivered in typical Lily style. She'd lived high and she'd fallen low. Now she was back.

She dipped her head, exposing the long graceful line of her neck. Tiny wisps of hair, almost like angel fluff, begged to be touched where they curled against her nape. Without thought, Jack did just that. Winding one of the whirls around his index finger, stroking its softness with his thumb. He felt, rather than saw, the goose bumps raise up on her skin.

"No, nothing too serious. Besides, I'm fine now." Her

voice stuttered slightly, as if she wasn't quite sure—or instead, as if his touch had unsettled her about as much as it was unsettling him. "Actually, as surprised as you all seem to be to see me here, I was more surprised to see Jack." Lily turned slightly to face him. "You were more driven to leave Onemata than I was. And here we are—most of us from high school—still here."

The silence that descended upon the group was uncomfortable. All eyes turned to Jack. Abruptly he let go of the strand of hair.

Was she really that ill-informed that she didn't know why he'd stayed? Why he hadn't pursued his dream and left the town they'd both found stifling? Anger roiled deep in his gut. How could she not know about his father's death, about her own father's hand in what came after? Or was she applying her own special brand of torture in the way that only a Fontaine could? He would show her who was in charge. Before he could say anything, however, a clutch of his guests made their excuses and headed off. Once a few had gone, the rest soon followed until eventually it was only Lily and Jack left.

"Come on." He rose to his feet in a shower of sand. "Let's go for a walk."

"I should be going to. It's getting late."

"It's just a walk," he coaxed.

Silently, Lily placed her hand in his and he enveloped her slender digits in his own much larger ones, pulling her to her feet. He hooked her against his body. Without those sexy ice picks on her feet she fit perfectly against his side. His body remembered hers as if it were only yesterday they'd been together instead of a decade ago.

The tide was out and the moon gleamed like a far-flung silver orb in the sky, sending glimmering light across the wet sand.

"Jack? Did I say something wrong back there?" Lily asked carefully. "I seem to have generated a mass exodus of your guests."

"You really don't know?" he answered, forcing himself to keep the anger from his tone of voice.

"Know what? Obviously I put my foot in it, judging by everyone's reaction."

Jack turned her in his arms so that her body lined up against his. "I had to stay. My father died."

Her soft cry of distress pierced his chest. She really hadn't known. He supposed that while she had been up in Auckland, getting ready to give away their child, a short piece in the national newspaper detailing a road fatality was insignificant. Rage boiled beneath the surface.

"I'm sorry, Jack. I had no idea. You must miss him very much." She lifted her hand to stroke his cheek with the back of her fingers. His skin burned at her touch.

"We got through it."

The words didn't do justice to the pain his family had gone through, not only at the loss of their much loved father and husband, but the financial strain had been immense. Charles Fontaine had annihilated his father—both personally and professionally—and then, with his lies, he'd systematically removed every last defence the Dolan family had had to survive.

As the oldest of four kids, most of the responsibility had fallen on Jack's twenty-year-old shoulders. It was a weight he'd willingly taken on, sure in the knowledge that one day providence would come full circle. That circle was just about complete.

"It must have been hell for you. All of you," Lily commiserated, her voice soft, her breath a light caress against his throat.

"Hell would be a picnic by comparison."

She had no idea. But she would. Very soon, she would.

It was time to put phase two of his plan into action. Let the seduction begin.

Jack pulled her more firmly against him, cradling her against his hips. He bent his head and took her lips with a kiss that sent a sizzling line of heat through his body. She tasted of smoky marshmallow and good wine, of the past and of forbidden love. He captured her lower lip and drew it softly between his, grazing it gently with his teeth. Her body melted against him and his deepening want for her grew hard and heavy. He swept his tongue across the lightly abraded surface of her lower lip and her mouth parted, giving him free entry into the soft recess beyond. Her tongue met his, taste for taste, probe for probe.

He fought to remind himself why he was doing this, to remain in total control, but his body reacted on a far baser level. It recognised the feel of her, the line of her frame as it pressed against his. The V of her groin as her heat burned through the clothing they wore and seeped into his skin as insidiously as his need for her had ruled his life before.

He slid one hand across the bare skin of her belly, his fingers tangling in the jewelled belly bar that had tormented him with its winking reminder of the softly rounded surface of her lightly tanned skin. He'd recognised her strategy in dressing the way she had from the minute she'd set foot through the front door, in the way she'd flirted and teased with his guests but remained aloof. "You can look but don't touch" had been all but imprinted on her forehead. As if she was better than the rest of them.

All night his hands had itched to slide inside the deep cowl of the halter neckline and caress her breasts, to prise away the fabric and lower his lips to the crest. To take her nipple into his mouth and wait for her gasp of need—of her desire for him.

Following the path of his thoughts he did exactly that, his fingers questing inside her neckline. A rush of satisfaction bloomed in his mind as his fingertips found her nipple, already hard and pointed. He brushed the flat of his palm against the sensitive peak. She arched against his hand with a throaty sigh, pressing harder, seeking more.

Jack curved his free arm around her waist, supporting her as he lifted his face from hers and trailed a line of kisses down her throat, working inexorably to his intended target. Her hands clutched at his shoulders as she arched further back, giving him full access, offering herself to him in the moonlight.

Her skin, which had been gilded with the golden light of the fire only moments ago, now gleamed with the caress of the moon's silver reflection. But instead of being cold, as the silver tint would have suggested, her skin was searingly hot. Hot and enticing and exuding a subtle fragrance—a blend of sweet and spicy perfume and the scent of pure Lily—that wound through his senses and deep into his heart.

When his lips closed over their prize he felt the shudder ripple through her body. He pulled with his tongue, drawing the tight bead further into his mouth, nibbling gently with his teeth until she finally released the gasp he recognised as her surrender. Her legs buckled slightly and he was forced to brace his legs further apart to support them both. The change in position put his aching arousal directly at her core. He flexed his hips against her, then laved his tongue across her nipple again and again before tracing a line under the curve of her breast where he knew she was incredibly sensitive.

Lily's hands left his shoulders and he felt her working at the knot that bound her halter top at the nape of her neck. Suddenly, with a sultry slither of cloth, both her breasts were bared to his sensual assault.

He didn't aim to disappoint her silent plea. He transferred his attentions to her other breast, affording the nipple the same tortuous attention as he had its twin.

His heart pounded in his chest and he could feel the answering beat of hers in the pulse at her neck as he let go her nipple and pressed his lips beneath her ear, hitting every erogenous zone in her upper body he remembered.

"Let's take this inside," he growled. He was so achingly hard it would be a killer to make the short walk back to the house, but what he had planned demanded more finesse than a quick romp in the sand. He wanted Lily boneless with need, limp with pleasure. Totally at his command.

Lily stiffened with awareness as his words filtered through the layers of desire that clouded her mind. Her body shrieked, *"Yes!"* Already he'd brought her so close to climax with his touch, with his lips, with the hard pressure of his arousal against her aching core. He'd forgotten nothing about what turned her on. But her clouded instincts warned her to pull back as the reality of her uninhibited behaviour with him, a man she'd sworn to herself not to trust again, closed in on her with suffocating reality.

"N-no," she stuttered as she lifted shaking hands to retie her halter top. It was lopsided but right now she didn't care. Right now all she wanted was to get away—fast. "I'm sorry, Jack. I shouldn't have let you do that—led you on like that. I…"

Lost for words, she turned and dashed through the sand as fast as the loose purchase would let her.

"No need to run, Lily. I'm not going to force you into anything you don't want." His voice carried across the sand, straight to her soul.

And that was the trouble. She did want him. Badly. So badly she hesitated for an infinitesimal moment. It was long enough for Jack to catch up with her.

"We're not strangers, Lily." His voice was soft, almost enticing, as if he was putting every ounce of persuasion he could into its tone and bend her to his will. "We used to be so good together. We can be again. No strings."

She should never have let him catch up. She knew if he touched her she'd capitulate, no matter how much she felt he'd let her down. She was an adult. Capable of making her own decisions. Capable of choosing her own lovers to satisfy her needs. And right now she needed him with all of the aching teenage angst that had resided in a black hole where her heart used to beat only for him. He was waiting for her answer and she had made her decision.

"No, Jack. We're not strangers. And that's exactly why I'm leaving now. Thank you for tonight." She hesitated and fired him the inscrutable smile she'd spent years perfecting. "For everything, tonight."

His pupils dilated, consuming the amber glow of his irises that reflected the dying fire. She saw the muscle working in his jaw as he absorbed the deliberate hit.

"You haven't changed a bit, have you?" A humourless smile crept across his face and his gaze narrowed.

"Changed? Yeah, I've changed. A lot, actually. Enough to know when to walk away from something or someone before things get out of hand—before someone gets hurt."

"Walk, Lily? We both know that's not your style." Bitter vitriol stained his next words. "You run. Just like you always did. To me. From me. It makes no difference. Deep down, where it counts, you haven't changed at all. You're still a spoiled irresponsible tease who puts her needs first and acts without consideration of her actions. Frankly, it's time you grew up."

He picked up her evening bag and shoes from where she'd left them by the fireside.

"Here. You'll need these."

She accepted them in silence and made her way around the bottom level of the house to where her car stood on its own in the wide turning bay. His words rang in her ears. How dare he accuse her of being spoiled? Of being a tease. She hadn't started that scene on the beach. She'd ended it. Just like she'd end it if the situation that had flared between them ever rose again—wouldn't she?

Five

The next morning saw Lily in absolute turmoil. She didn't know whether to be furious with Jack or whether to just get back in her car, knock down his door and jump into his arms to rid herself of the sexual hunger he'd reawakened in her.

She headed into her shower in an attempt to tamp down some of that heat. She'd thought she was in control. That she'd made a conscious choice. First to go to his home last night, and second to allow him to kiss her and start to make love to her the way he did.

She'd wanted him every bit as much as he had obviously wanted her. The problem was, what happened after that? Where would that leave them both? Sure, she might be able to go some way to assuaging the ache deep down inside, she could even manage to rid herself of all the what-might-have-been questions she'd been riddled with since she'd left. But what if she ended up wanting him more, needing him more? What if she still loved him?

Lily turned off the faucet and dried herself slowly. Still in love with Jack Dolan? The thought struck sheer terror to her heart. No. She couldn't still love Jack Dolan. There was too much water under the bridge. She'd carved his memory from her soul on the day she'd buried Nathaniel. It was the last time she'd allowed herself to weep for their lost love.

Putting that behind her had been the hardest thing she'd ever had to deal with in her life next to losing their baby. But she'd managed both on her own. She'd rebuilt her life, made her mistakes and learned from them.

As Lily knotted the towel across her breasts and began to apply a light sheen of makeup with a practiced hand, she thought back to the recent catastrophe—all because she'd trusted her accountant as her financial adviser. She'd allowed friendly familiarity to sway her better judgement. Okay, so she'd made some bad choices, but she could start again. Reinvent Lily Fontaine. The thing was, there was little call for a washed-up model who'd left behind a reputation for unreliability and unsavoury company.

How different would her life have been if the plans she and Jack had made all those years ago had come to fruition? Would they still be together? Would he be the cold, calculating man who'd lambasted her last night or would he have simply been an older version of the boy she'd fallen in love with when she was sixteen and he only eighteen years old?

Who knew? And what difference did it make anyway? She'd seen the man he was now and she was still wildly attracted to him. That she could identify it and analyse it would stand her in good stead in the coming weeks. They were bound to cross paths, and maybe sleeping with him would get him out of her system, once and for all. Of one thing, though, she was certain. If or when she did go to bed with Jack Dolan, it would be on her terms and because *she* wanted to.

He'd been so angry last night. Almost vibrating with fury. Unrequited lust? Maybe. She knew she'd been totally out of line. She'd allowed herself to be bowled over by sensation, divorcing reason from feeling. And oh, what feelings he'd evoked in her. Being in Jack's arms had left her mind devoid of thought for her actions. All she'd wanted to do was to dwell in sensation, in the familiarity—yet newness—of his touch.

She'd had other lovers, not as many as the gossip mags cared to suggest, but enough to know that the way her body ignited for him was a one in a million reaction. A reaction that still had her skin tingling with the memory of his touch as she put on her underwear and dressed in a soft, pale-blue T-shirt and denim skirt. Determined to put him out of her thoughts for the rest of the day, Lily went downstairs to get some breakfast.

In the kitchen she was surprised to see her father still settled at the breakfast bar, a mug of coffee in one hand, a financial report in the other and a roll of antacid tablets on the counter in front of him.

"Morning, Dad. You're late leaving for work today."

Lily dropped a perfunctory kiss on her father's forehead. "How's the coffee?"

"Strong. Just the way I like it." He barely even looked up from the papers, a frown furrowed his brow.

"You're not having anything to eat?"

"No. I'll be fine." He gave the papers one last rustle then laid them facedown on the kitchen bench. "You were late home last night."

So that explained why he was still here. Time for the age-old inquisition. Lily felt herself bristle. She'd lived on her own for so long it felt strange to be responsible to someone else. She bit back the retort that sprang to her lips. She was altogether too sensitive and too reactive these days. It was what always got her into trouble. From today she was turning over a new leaf. Think first then speak.

"Sorry if I disturbed you when I came in. I tried to be quiet." She poured herself a coffee from the carafe on the hot plate then grabbed some eggs from the fridge. Beating them to a frothy mess would go some way to alleviating the frustration she felt right now. "Are you sure I can't get you something? You shouldn't head off to the office on just a coffee."

"You didn't disturb me. I was working. And no, I'll get the restaurant to send me something over later today."

"Working at home as well as all the hours you're putting in lately? I've hardly seen you since I got back, Dad. Is everything okay at FonCom? Is there anything I can do?"

His guffaw startled her. "Do, Lily?" He shook his head. "No, my girl. There's nothing you can do. Just stay out of trouble and we'll both be fine."

He could reduce her to feeling like a teenager just like that. Lily gritted her teeth. Moving back home was never going to be easy. Her dad had always tried to run her life before. He probably planned on simply picking up where he left off.

"Well, I'd best be on my way." He grabbed the roll of antacid tablets and shoved them in his trouser's pocket. "Remember what I said yesterday, Lily. Stay away from Jack Dolan. He's always been trouble for this family. All the Dolans have."

"Dad, that's an unfair comment. You know that. You and Jack's dad worked together for years. I didn't know he'd passed away."

Inwardly, Lily groaned. So much for the "think first" thing. It had lasted…what, all of three minutes? She saw her father's posture stiffen.

"And why would you know that?"

"Just something someone said last night," Lily evaded as she bent to get a bowl from the cupboard to whip her eggs in.

"Someone who?"

He'd always had a knack for knowing when he wasn't being told the full story and Lily knew he wouldn't let things lie until he had it from her now. She sucked in a deep breath.

"Jack. I heard it from Jack, Dad. Okay?"

"So he was there at the barbecue last night." Charles Fontaine snorted in disgust. "If he so much as lays one hand on you again, I'll—"

"Dad! I'm not a baby anymore." Heat rose in Lily's cheeks, half in anger and half in embarrassment at her father's words. It had been more than a hand that Jack had laid on her last night and she'd welcomed him. Lord, if her father only knew, he'd be apoplectic. Actually, far better that he didn't know. Ever. "I can take care of myself, truly. I know how to handle his type. And for the record, before you hear it from anyone else, the barbecue last night was at his house."

She tensed, waiting for her father's reaction. She wasn't disappointed. For the next five minutes he raged on about how foolish she was to have gone in the first place, and that she could rethink her options if she thought he was going to provide her with a home just so she could ruin her life all over again. His colour had become an alarming shade of purple.

"Dad, please, calm down. It's not like you think. Jack and I are bound to bump into one another. Onemata's not so huge that we can avoid each other completely. We can be adult about this, and if that means seeing one another socially from time to time, then that's what we'll do. If you're not happy with that, I'll find somewhere else to stay."

"Over my dead body. This is your home. It's where you belong and it's where you'll stay."

Charles looked as though he was about to say something else but the trill of his cell phone interrupted him. "Yes!" he snapped, "I'm on my way." He slid his phone back in his pocket and gave Lily one last glare. "Mark my words, missy. He'll just lead you into trouble again. Stay away from him. Well away."

Lily sat at the breakfast bar until the house was completely silent. Why had she even bothered to try to defend seeing Jack again? It had always been like that with her father. Always at odds. Him telling her what to do, her arguing back and running flat-out to Jack—partly for the comfort she knew he'd give her and partly because she'd known it would rile her father intensely. It had been her silent stab at independence, and had been as futile then as it was now.

Jack had been right. She did always run from her problems. She'd done it again simply by coming home instead of facing up to her responsibilities in Los Angeles. It was easier to run than to face things she didn't like, easier to put on a facade and pretend everything was okay. It had been living life on a knife edge.

It really was time to grow up.

She owed Jack an apology. She didn't like the fact, but if she was going to get control back in her life, really make something of herself, she had to start acting like the adult she always insisted she was.

Jack looked up from his computer as his secretary walked into his office with a smile wider than the Auckland Harbour Bridge pasted across her face and an enormous arrangement of colourful cut flowers in her arms. Lead settled uncomfortably in his gut. He recognised the flowers. He'd chosen the profusion of stems himself at the florist this morning before ordering them sent to Lily with an apology for his behaviour last night. He'd lost control, had lost sight of his goal and had lashed out verbally in reaction to the near overwhelming physical magnetism between them and her outright rejection of it.

Now, it appeared, he'd given her a platform from which to reject him again. The thought left a sour taste in his mouth. One he had every intention of overruling at the earliest opportunity.

"Don't bother putting them down in here, Sandy. Take them home or throw them out, I don't care."

"But, Jack, they're addressed to you." Her smile grew impossibly even wider.

"What are you talking about?" He'd written the card and envelope himself, even tucked the flap inside the envelope to close it before handing it to the florist.

"Here." Sandy pulled the card from the arrangement and handed it to him. "Read it yourself."

Jack took the small envelope from her. Sure enough, his handwriting listing Lily's address had been neatly crossed out and his office address written in its place. No wonder Sandy was just about shaking with barely concealed laughter. A flash of irritation swept through him.

"That'll be all, thank you, Sandy." His voice was clipped, his instruction clear in its tone.

"And the flowers?"

"Leave them here for now. They will be going back out again shortly. Call the courier and—" He broke off, a grim smile curving his lips. "Forget the courier. I'll take them myself. I'll be back in about an hour."

Jack drew his Crossfire SRT-6 Roadster to a halt in front of Charles Fontaine's house with a spray of fine gravel from under the low-profile tyres. He hooked up the arrangement from the floor of the passenger side of the car and stalked to the front door.

No one refused to accept an apology from Jack

Dolan, especially not Lily Fontaine. The fact that his attempt at apology hadn't exactly been driven by sincerity challenged his sense of honour. He'd never apologised and not genuinely meant it before, but Lily had a way of making him walk outside his firmly drawn lines and he didn't like it one bit. Eschewing the doorbell, Jack hammered a clenched fist on the heavy wooden front door.

His heart did an uncomfortable flip in his chest as the door opened, revealing a version of Lily that put him more in mind of the girl he'd lost his heart to as a hormone-driven teenager. Her hair was loose today, much shorter than it used to be, and barely touched her shoulders in a swathe of soft curls. She was barefoot and for some reason the sight of her pearl-pink-painted toenails lent her a vulnerability that spoke to him at his basest caveman level. Something of what he was feeling must have shown in his face because he was suddenly arrested by the expression in her eyes, which flashed like blue flame.

"These are yours." He thrust the flowers in her arms. "Don't send them back again." He strode back to the car, crunching the gravel underfoot with a satisfying sound.

"Jack?"

He halted at the door of his car. "What?"

"Did you read the card?"

"Of course I read the card. I wrote it. You sent it back." He crossed his arms in front of him.

Lily slipped the card out of the arrangement and put the flowers down on the tiled floor. The action made her denim skirt ride further up the back of her thighs, exposing a length of leg that sent a message of considerable demand from his groin to his head. She straightened and walked toward him, the rough texture of the driveway obviously causing discomfort to her unclad feet.

"Here, read it."

In bristling silence Jack took the envelope from her and slid his finger under the sealed flap to rip it open. For a brief moment he allowed himself to imagine her tongue as it might have caressed the edge of the flap, moistening it to close it down. He quickly scanned the contents.

"Couldn't you have just rung me and said yes?"

A small smile played around her lips, a teasing smile—one he had the almost overwhelming urge to control with his kiss.

"I suppose I could have, but I thought this would probably say it better. I had no need to accept your apology, you were due one from me. I behaved childishly last night, Jack. You were right, I do run away from things when it gets rough." The smile slipped from her face and her expression was replaced with a far more sombre look.

Was she thinking about when she'd left him the first time? About their child? Since he'd found out about the private adoption Charles Fontaine had arranged, and which Lily had countersigned in agreement, he'd barely been able to think of anything else. Somewhere out there a stranger was raising his child—a stranger his son or daughter called Dad. His stomach knotted painfully. *That's why you're here,* he reminded himself. *Revenge with benefits.*

"I'll take that as an acceptance of my invitation?" he pressed. He fought to keep his tone even, determined not to betray the direction of his thoughts, and watched her eyes carefully for any sign of duplicity.

"Yeah," she said softly. "I won't run away again. I'd love to spend the day out with you on your boat. It would be great."

Yes! Jack allowed her answer to wash over him in exultant waves.

"I'll pick you up on Friday at 9:00 a.m. then." He opened his car door and dropped into the seat.

"Could I meet you at the marina?"

Her voice sounded uncertain and he guessed her concern straight away.

"Afraid of what your father will say, Lily?"

"Let me take this in baby steps, Jack. While I'm under his roof I don't want to antagonise him any more than necessary. He's already under a lot of strain."

Sure he was, Jack thought grimly. The strain of trying to hold together a business that was overstretched fiscally and had steadily diminishing staff resources. He could afford to let Lily take baby steps with this one although the analogy was anathema to him—ultimately the prize would be his.

"Okay, there's parking at the marina for visitors. Meet me on Pier 23, berth 7. Same time."

"I'll be there," she promised.

"And don't have breakfast. We'll have something while we're out, okay?"

Jack slid his sunglasses onto his face and gave her a smile in farewell before putting his car into gear and driving carefully around the turning bay and out up the drive. Anticipation swelled deep inside. A day. A whole day. The possibilities were endless.

Six

Friday morning dawned with one of those crystal-clear summer days where you felt as if you could see forever. The heat was already building and Lily dressed carefully, wary of the southern hemisphere's heightened risk of UV damage. The white muslin blouse she wore over her bikini would provide some additional protection to the sunblock she'd already liberally coated herself with.

Into a large beach bag she shoved her towel and a change of clothing, then pulled on a pair of denim cutoffs she'd found in her old dresser drawer and slid her feet into rubber-soled shoes.

Since her altercation with her father two days ago she'd barely seen him. He'd arrived home each evening, collected the meal that Mrs. Manson had cooked and left for him in the oven, then secreted himself away in his office. Most nights Lily hadn't even heard him come upstairs to bed.

For herself she'd started to get into a wellness routine to get back in shape, which began each morning with a run along the beach—half the time expecting to see Jack on his deck as she had earlier in the week. But she hadn't seen him again since the day he'd come over with the flowers.

She smiled to herself as she lifted the beach tote. He'd been so insulted that she'd returned them. At the time she'd thought it was a nifty idea. Her pulse quickened in anticipation of seeing him today. She hesitated a moment while she checked her reflection in the mirror. It had been one of her deepest fears, bumping into him again. He'd been the major reason why she'd chosen to stay away for all this time, and here she was, planning to spend a whole day with him. Anyone else would think she was certifiable.

Maybe she was, Lily decided as she went through to the garage and got into her car. She'd never in a million years have imagined she'd be like this—looking forward to seeing Jack with an eagerness that had her blood bubbling in her veins with excitement.

She was early at the marina and as she alighted from her car she looked around. Progress had certainly not bypassed Onemata if the rows of boats and the wealth of water-going craft were anything to go by. She counted along the piers, finding number twenty-three, and walked along until she reached berth seven where a huge, luxury power boat nestled between two fingerlike jetties.

She hitched her tote higher on her shoulder, suddenly assailed with nerves. She knew Jack was successful, she'd even read articles about him in the States, about his Midas touch in business management strategies, but this, like his home, was a bold physical statement of his wealth and standing.

She had grown up with money and lived a very moneyed lifestyle at the peak of her career. She recognised serious financial accomplishment when she saw it.

"Hey, come aboard."

Her heart stuttered in her chest as she heard Jack call out to her from the flybridge. In an instant he'd come down the gently curved stairs and was on the main deck. Lily jumped lightly from the jetty to the transom at the back of the boat, skirting the small inflatable dinghy secured there.

"I think this one is more my size," she said with a nervous laugh.

"Really, I thought you'd be blasé about this kind of thing by now." Jack crossed his arms and her eyes were drawn immediately to the sprinkling of dark hair across his strong forearms and the way his navy polo shirt stretched across his shoulders. A light wind tugged at his hair, tousling the controlled and highly groomed look he favoured these days, and reducing him to more like the young man she'd known.

"Blasé? No, not about this." Lily gestured to the dinghy. "So, what's the little one for?"

"To get us to the beach."

"Beach? Which one?"

"It's a surprise. Relax, you'll enjoy it. Go stow your things inside and come up top with me."

Lily did as he bade, taking a moment to appreciate

the plush interior of the boat and the modern fittings in the galley. It really was a home away from home. He certainly had come up in the world. She put her bag on one of the deep comfortable seats fitted against the hull and climbed up to the flybridge where Jack waited.

"She's beautiful," Lily commented, trailing a hand over the highly polished railing. "Do you get out much?"

"Not as often as I'd like lately, but that's about to change. I'm reaching the end of a time-consuming project. Once that's all done, I'll be able to kick back and relax a bit more."

He smiled at her, but Lily noticed some strain around his eyes and his smile seemed forced. Brushing it off as her being oversensitive, she settled back in the seat next to Jack's and resolved to stop looking for trouble. It was a glorious day and she was out on a spectacular boat with a handsome man. What more could a woman want? Butterflies fluttered in her tummy as she watched Jack expertly manoeuvre the large vessel from its berth and out of the marina. His hands were large and capable on the controls and a frisson of expectation shivered down the length of her spine as she remembered the feel of those hands as he'd caressed her body only a couple of nights ago.

Since then she'd found herself thinking of Jack at odd moments of the day—each thought, each memory winding the knot of tension inside her tighter and tighter. A tension she recognised all too well as being powerfully physical in its demand. She forced her gaze away from him, to the vista of the ocean in front and the coastline that sped away to the side of them.

She wasn't stupid. The time would come again when they came together. With the way they had all but fused together with the heat of their passion the other night, it was inevitable. And when they did, maybe—just maybe—it'd heal the hollow that echoed deep inside and allow her to effectively move on with her life.

Jack watched Lily as she relaxed in her seat. With her hair blown back by the breeze and her face tilted to the sun, she could have been posing for a photo shoot. The thin material of her blouse hinted at the shadows and valleys of her body, in its own way revealing more than it covered as the wind plastered it against her slender form, accentuating her feminine curves. He could almost fool himself that he was growing accustomed to his body's instant reaction to hers. The discomfort of walking around in a semi-aroused state while he was around her was a small price to pay for the satisfaction that was his due.

He hadn't been kidding when he'd said he'd be spending more time on the boat once he'd completed his "project." In fact he looked forward to that moment with increasing anticipation. In a few weeks it would be the tenth anniversary of his father's death—Jack's self-appointed deadline to exact the revenge that was due against Charles Fontaine.

Yes, today was going to be productive in its own way. Wooing Lily, removing the last of the barriers she may have between them so he could fulfil this additional yet incredibly sweet reprisal, would be deeply satisfying. His body tightened. The countdown had begun.

After about half an hour's ride down the coast Jack slowed the engines and turned inland, guiding the boat into a sheltered bay that nestled in a golden semi-circle at the bottom of a steep cliff. Access to the beach appeared only to be from the water, although they'd traversed the rocks once, many years ago, to reach this destination once before. He wondered if she remembered.

Little had changed since their first visit here, except, perhaps, for their mode of transport to get there. Back then they'd ridden miles on the coast road on his motorbike, then clambered over the rocks on the outgoing tide to the tiny private bay. Jack shot her a glance, gauging to see if she recognised the beach.

Dawning realisation sent a blush of colour into her cheeks. Yeah, she remembered, all right. Jack savoured the satisfaction. The memories would serve as an effective seasoning to his plans for the day. He set the engines to idle while the anchor lowered and he checked to make certain the boat was secure before shutting the engines off completely.

"Come on down. I promised you breakfast, you must be starving."

He shot down the stairs before her, turning to watch as she descended behind him. His eyes devoured her long tanned legs as she made her way slowly down the stairs and his body hardened. Today was going to be torture. It would be worth it, he reminded himself. Nothing in his life had come easily so far and he didn't expect that to change anytime soon. He reached out strong hands to her waist and lifted her down the last of the stairs, letting his hands slide up her rib cage, his palms heated by the texture of her skin through her flimsy blouse before he let her go.

"Thank you." She smiled and ducked her head as if she was suddenly shy.

"Any time," he murmured, his voice low, his hands tingling from the contact.

Her body's reaction didn't go unseen by his sharp gaze and he smiled to himself as he recognised the tight beading of her nipples beneath the lycra top of her bikini. Perfect. At least he wasn't the only one experiencing a little discomfort.

They walked into the cabin and Jack went down the few carpet-covered stairs that led to the galley.

"Is there anything I can do to help?" Lily asked.

He could feel her, standing close behind him. If he turned he'd likely be able to take her in his arms without a single protest. But then, where would the fun of the chase be, the cat and mouse, the delight of suspenseful expectation?

"There's a sideboard built in over there." He gestured toward a gently curved wooden cupboard hugging the interior wall of the boat. "Grab a couple of trays, placemats and knives and forks. I'll do the rest."

By the time he'd whipped up a couple of Spanish omelettes Lily had the trays ready and was standing on the rear deck looking out at the sparkling ocean. From the back she still looked like she had as a teenager. Long slender legs, delicate shoulders and an impossibly long neck supporting her blond head. It wasn't until you got closer, he acknowledged, that you saw just how the past ten years had changed Lily. There was a wariness in her eyes that she'd never had before, a reticence that implied she wasn't quite as impulsive as the girl she'd been. It was that same caution that had seen her break away from him the other night and that had alerted him to the fact he needed to tread carefully if he was going to achieve his goal.

Today was going to be approached from an entirely different angle. Softly. Enticingly. He was going to make sure she wanted him with a hunger and a burning need that would play her straight into his hands.

"Breakfast's up," he called as he put the two warmed plates on the waiting trays and lifted the trays to carry them out. "I hope you still like mushrooms."

Lily spun around with a smile to accept her tray. "Yeah, I do, thanks."

They sat at the back of the boat, barely moving in the calm bay.

"Oh, this is good!" she exclaimed after taking a forkful of the fluffy mixture into her mouth. "Where on earth did you learn to cook like this?"

"I picked up a lot from Mum, after Dad died, but for the most part it's been trial and error. I never wanted to be one of those men who relied on take-out or TV dinners."

"Well, you've definitely graduated beyond those. This is divine."

Jack watched as Lily took another mouthful, her lips glistening slightly in the morning light and the smooth muscles in her throat working rhythmically as she swallowed. The urge to press his mouth to her skin, to feel the movement of her throat, to taste her lips, swelled from deep inside him. Suddenly aware of his intent gaze, Lily stopped, fork midair, before taking another bite.

"What is it?" she asked, her voice breathless, her eyes flaring as she met his gaze.

For a moment he could say nothing but then rational thought kicked back in.

"Nothing. It's good to see you're enjoying the meal." And that's all, he censured himself. For now.

After they'd cleared away the breakfast dishes, a job that only took a few minutes, Jack took Lily on a tour of the boat.

"This is amazing," she said as she inspected the two miniature bathrooms off the separate staterooms on the lower deck. "Who designs these things?"

"You remember my younger brother, Finn? He did the interior design work. He has his own business north of Auckland. They design and fit interiors for all marine applications although most of his work is private luxury craft like this. He's doing well."

"I'm not surprised if this is anything to go by."

Lily stepped into the main stateroom, hovering in the doorway as she took in the expanse of the bed that dominated the space.

"They've thought of everything, haven't they? Do you spend much time out overnight?"

Jack smiled. There was a catch to her voice that hinted at the possibility that she was envisaging the same fantasy as he was right now. Their bodies, bathed in moonlight from the side windows and the skylight above, entwined together.

"Not as often as I'd like to. But that will change soon. Come on, let's head to the beach."

Back on the main deck Jack loaded a sun umbrella

and folded straw mats into the inflatable dinghy together with a large cooler bag and her tote before sliding the smaller craft into the water.

"More food?" Lily teased as he handed her into the dinghy.

"We are here for the day. A man's gotta eat." Jack joked back, suddenly struck by how comfortable he was with her. It would be all too easy to lose sight of his goal, to let things between them develop naturally without an ulterior motive in mind. He needed to stay on track. It all came down to timing.

At the beach, Lily helped Jack pull the dinghy up the sand, clear of the lapping water. She couldn't believe he'd brought her back here. She looked around, noting that the beach had changed some since their last visit. More of the sandstone rock had been worn away by the unrelenting movement of the sea, a couple of old trees had tumbled off the eroding cliff face and lay in a tangled mess of dead wood at the base.

She still remembered their last visit as if it were yesterday. Her backside had ached from the time they'd spent on the bike, and Jack had laughed at her, teasing her about how "soft" she was. He'd told her he'd make it all better. And he had. He'd led her around the rocks, holding her hand through the more precarious parts and laughing at her squeals of fear at the waves as they crashed close by.

The discovery of a huge rock pool, the size of a small swimming pool, had seen him strip himself of his clothing and dive in. She still remembered how breathless she'd been. It was the first time she'd seen him completely naked and the firm chiselled lines of his body had taken her breath away.

He'd eventually persuaded her to follow him into the water, and she had. She still remembered the tense knot of nerves in her stomach as she'd unbuttoned her shirt and shrugged it off her shoulders. He'd watched every tiny movement as she'd slowly divested herself of her shirt and then her jeans, standing there in only her bra and undies, feeling incredibly vulnerable until she'd seen the look in his eyes. The look that had made her feel as though she was the most beautiful creature in all the world. The look that had seen her remove her underwear and gently slide into the water and glide toward him until she was close enough to wrap her arms and legs around him.

She still remembered vividly the sensation of his naked body against her skin. The water had been silken cool, but he'd been hot, so hot. He'd treaded water for both of them as they'd kissed with all the passion and hunger that months of restraint had built up. The snatched moments they'd shared together outside of school hours and his work at the petrol station faded into nothing in comparison to what they'd shared that day.

Lily fought a groan as lightning-hot need scored through her body at the memory. As if he knew exactly what path her thoughts were taking, Jack spoke.

"The rock pool's still there. Remember that day?"

"A girl never forgets her first time, Jack." She opted for a flip response, her emotions too raw to be openly acknowledged. Not here. Not now. Not when she was still so unsure of why she'd even chosen to be with him today.

"Nor does a guy."

Seven

She whipped her head around at the four small words, quietly spoken. The expression on his face struck straight to Lily's heart, making her gasp.

"Jack?" She took a step toward him, to where he stood—his bare feet planted firmly in the sand.

"The past's the past," he said abruptly. "Let's leave it there for now."

Lily nodded. Her body tingled all over with the flood of memories. They'd spent some time fooling in the rock pool before making their way off the rocks to the sandy cove where they now stood. It was there they'd made love for the first time. She'd never known it had been his first time, too. He'd been so tender with her, so reverent. She'd felt so incredibly special, as if she was the most precious thing in his world.

How times changed, she reminded herself. He was right. It was better to leave the past in the past rather than let bitter disappointment and reproach colour what promised to be a spectacular day.

She helped Jack unpack the sun umbrella and mats from the dinghy and spread the mats out on the sand. It was getting warmer and once they were set up Lily pulled off her blouse and shorts and raced for the water.

"Last one in is a rotten egg!" she shouted.

"Cheat!" Jack's voice sounded a lot closer than she expected.

As she reached the water's edge she heard his pounding feet running up behind her. She put on a burst of speed, but he was quicker and his body flew past hers, cleaving the water beside her before she could dive in.

Strong hands circled her ankles and tugged her off balance, and she fell backward into the water, still laughing. She surfaced and wiped her hair back off her face.

"Hey, that wasn't fair play!" She smiled.

"No, it wasn't. But fair play never got anyone anywhere in this world."

Jack's expression was enigmatic and Lily was tempted to answer until she noticed the tattoo on his chest. She lifted her hand to touch it, then let her hand drop back to the water.

"You still have it," she said quietly.

Jack absently stroked the outline of the lily he'd had indelibly marked over his heart to acknowledge the first time they'd made love.

"Yeah."

Abruptly he dove back under the water, resurfacing some distance away and swimming parallel to the beach with strong, steady strokes. For a while Lily simply watched him, admiring the power and the strength he displayed in the water. He'd always been tall, and slightly on the lean side, but maturity had put more muscle on his frame and imbued him with a masculinity that couldn't be questioned.

Lily flipped over onto her back and floated for a while, simply enjoying the peace of the ocean and the sheer luxury of being able to relax and enjoy herself. It had been a while since she'd taken time out and chosen just to do nothing. The past few years had taken their toll—from the giddy heights of being the darling of the fashion house she'd represented to the depths of despair when her recovery had been so slow and she'd been unable to fulfil the terms of her contract. Fighting her way back into her former position had been like trying to conquer a vertical glacier in a pair of slippers and a dressing gown. Futile.

And what did she have left to show for any of it? Nothing bar a few designer gowns that she'd probably sell anyway. She'd lived the life expected of her, been seen in the right places with the right people—all of which had taken a financial toll that had sunk her in the end.

It was a time to rebuild and replenish. Grow up. Everybody had to learn sometime. Her time had come. Thinking about selling her designer clothing suddenly triggered off an idea. Most of the stores in Onemata catered for more casual beach wear. Anyone wanting to get anything more formal or dressy usually had it made or took a trip up to Auckland. With the change in population in the town and the new business centre there would be increasing demand for more upmarket clothing for both men and women. She could do that. She could source and supply ranges for both. Ideas tumbled through her mind and excitement bubbled in her veins. She could make this work—really work. She couldn't wait to discuss it with her father. She'd need his help, initially, to get her idea off the ground, but she'd pay him back, every last penny. Today was Friday, but come Monday she'd be checking out some retail space in town. She couldn't wait.

Lily rolled over in the water and began to swim back toward the beach. She realised that for the first time in forever, she was actually happy. She felt as though she was back in control of her life, and it was a darn fine feeling.

Jack was strolling along the shoreline toward her as Lily came out of the water.

"Enjoy your swim?" he asked.

"Yeah, I did. It's like it freed something in my mind. Something that's been stuck for a while."

"Oh? Nothing too painful, I hope?" A smile flashed across his face.

Lily laughed, the sound bubbling from her throat without inhibition. "No, nothing painful. Yet. I just had an idea of what to do with myself now I'm back for good."

"For good? Are you sure?"

"Yeah. I'm sure, now." She fell into step beside him as they walked up the beach to their things. "I've been drifting for too long. It feels good to have a direction again."

"I know what you mean. The things that drive you bring you far greater satisfaction in the long run."

He picked up his towel and dried his body. Lily averted her eyes. He was too much. Too close.

"What is it that drives you, Jack?" she asked, curious to find out what had burned in him so bright that he'd made such a success of his business exploits.

Jack shook out his towel and laid it on the mat in the sunshine. Her question hit him broadside. What would she say, he wondered, if she knew the truth? He lowered himself to the towel and lay on his side, propped up on one elbow, and looked up at Lily.

"A lot of things drove me in the past. Survival primarily. Nowadays, it's basically down to satisfaction." He watched her closely as she absorbed the information. A tiny frown of puzzlement creased her forehead before smoothing away again.

"Survival." She said the word emphatically, with no hint of question in her voice. "It was hard on all of you when your dad died, wasn't it?"

Jack reached for his sunglasses and slid them onto his face. Hard? The word didn't do their struggle justice. He gave Lily a wry smile.

"We got through it. The alternative wasn't an option. We didn't have anything or anyone else to fall back on."

"And you made it. Your mum must be really proud of you."

"She is."

Tania Dolan was incredibly, deeply proud. As his father would have been, also, if he had lived long enough to see what Jack had made of his life. If he had anything to thank Charles Fontaine for, it was giving him the tool to drive himself to succeed at all cost—and it had cost him dearly. But it would all be worth it in another week. Jack almost couldn't believe it was all coming to an end so soon. In just seven days FonCom would find out they'd lost the bid on another contract. The ripple effect of that lack of business, combined with the tactical decimation of the company to date, would send everything sliding toward a deep dark pit from which there would be no recovery.

Then, and only then, would Jack be satisfied.

Lily had stretched out on her towel beside him, and was reapplying sunblock. From behind the tinted shield of his sunglasses he watched as her hands stroked the cream down her legs, massaging it into the skin. A flush of heat prickled across his skin that had nothing to do with the sun and everything to do with need to replace her hands with his, to stroke, long and firm, over her thighs and down her legs and back up again. Maybe now would be a good time to go for another cooling swim, he thought as he rolled over onto his stomach to hide his semi-erection before it became full-blown.

"Do you need some sunblock? I can put some on your back if you'd like?"

Like? Yeah, he'd like, all right. What the hell? Why not?

"Thanks, that'd be great," he murmured, mentally bracing himself for the feel of her hands against his skin.

Jack felt her move closer, her knees almost touching his side as she shook some lotion into her hand. Just think of something else, he told himself as she lowered her hands to his lower back and started to work up his spine in sweeping strokes. There wasn't a visual image strong enough to douse the fiery trail her touch ignited across his skin. She'd warmed the lotion in her hands before applying it so he hadn't even had the advantage of cold shock on his skin to counteract the heat that burned throughout his body. Her hands, though slender, felt strong and smooth as she worked the sunblock into his skin, working it into his shoulders and down the backs of his arms.

"You've got some really hard knots here," Lily commented as she massaged the broad lines of his shoulders and across the base of his neck. "You want me to try to work them out?"

They weren't all that was hard, Jack groaned inwardly as she applied a firmer pressure to the knotted muscles. He heard a slight hitch in her breathing, the telltale sound a clue to how touching him was making her feel. He hoped she was experiencing the same torment he was. The same need for satisfaction. And satisfaction would come—at a price.

"Sure, have at them."

Jack knew her time was wasted but he wasn't averse to her contact. The tension in his shoulders wouldn't diminish until his plans all came together and Charles Fontaine was a broken man. As broken as his father had been.

By the time Lily started on the backs of his legs he was one massive ache that had nothing to do with knotted muscles and everything to do with wanting her with a hunger he fought to keep tamped down. Her slender fingers caressed his inner thighs as she ensured his skin was thoroughly protected. Jack clenched his teeth, hard.

"Lily?" He forced the word out and mercifully her hands slowed and stopped.

"Is something wrong?"

"You're killing me here." He turned his head to look at her, noting instantly the flush of peach across her cheeks and upper chest, the glitter in her eyes that he'd always found so incredibly sexy. No, she wasn't unmoved by their contact. In fact, he'd hazard to say that she was as uncomfortably aroused as he himself right now. It would be so easy to hook one arm around her tiny waist and draw her down beside him on the mat, to slide his leg over hers and to pin her beneath him and show her the full extent of his need for her right now.

"You want me to stop?" Her voice was breathless, her chest rising and falling rapidly, drawing his attention to her nipples pressed hard against the fabric of her bikini top.

"God, no. But if you don't, I won't be accountable for my actions." He managed a laugh. Strained but genuine.

The blush on her cheeks deepened as she took his meaning.

"Well, we can't have you losing control then, can we?" She smiled back, a hint of mischief in the play of her lips. She allowed her hand to trail up the back of one thigh before giving him a light slap on his backside.

Quick as lightening he'd flipped over and caught her hand, drawing her to him, against the hardness of his erection.

"Still want to play, Lily?" He challenged. His body throbbed as he waited for her reply. "Like the old days?"

She caught at her lower lip with her teeth, her pupils flaring, all but consuming the pale blue of her irises. Her fingers flexed against him, whether it was involuntarily or not he didn't know and didn't care. The sensations she kindled in him were exquisite, and he wanted more. He'd planned to keep today on an even keel. To tantalise, but above all to remain firmly in charge. Right now tantalising could go to hell and back. He wanted it all. He wanted her. Now.

A tiny sound escaped her mouth, and the pressure of her hand increased against his groin before she tugged free of his hold.

"This isn't a good idea, Jack. We shouldn't—" Lily pulled away from him, hugging her knees up to her chest and staring out at the water. "We were young then. Different people to who we are now." She barely made enough sound for him to catch the words.

"Yeah, you're right, we were young, and look where it got us last time." Lily shot him a sharp glance, confusion evident in her eyes at his comment. Clearly she'd expected him to argue her withdrawal. Force with a woman had never been his style, ever. "But we still want each other, and we're all grown up now. What are we going to do about that?"

"I don't know, Jack. I really don't know. I'm really confused right now. My life has imploded and to be honest I don't need any more complications. I need something solid beneath my feet. Something I can build a base on and get ahead with." She looked straight at him, tears in her eyes. "You're a major complication. What we had, what went wrong between us—I was too young to know what the right thing was to do. I still can't get a handle on it. But I do know I can't do that again. It would totally crush me."

Crush her? She barely knew the meaning. Did she realise he knew about their baby? Had she any idea how he'd felt when he'd finally found out the truth? On top of everything her father had done to his family, her deception was the bitterest pill. He waited for her to speak again, to see if she'd finally share the truth about her leaving the way she had that night. It was her perfect opportunity, but he waited in vain as she remained silent.

He chose his words carefully. "We can't deny we still have something together. You've been back less than a week and already we can't keep our hands off each other. Why don't we just take it one day at a time? No pressure. Just two old friends rediscovering each other." His last words soured on his tongue. Friends. They'd gone there and beyond. He still bore the scars on his heart to prove it.

She sighed. "Did you really mean it when we arrived at the beach? What you said about the past staying in the past?"

"If that's what it takes."

"Then, yes. I can do one day at a time. It's about all I'm capable of right now."

Jack put out his hand. "It's a deal then. One day at a time."

Lily tentatively put her hand in his. He maintained eye contact as he firmed his grip and drew her hand to his lips, pressing them to her knuckles.

Lily heaved a massive sigh of relief when he let her hand go again. Her heart pounded in her chest and her body still hummed with the build up of repressed sexual energy. The come-down from this was going to leave her shattered, both mentally and physically. She lacked the stamina to withstand such an assault on her senses.

To her surprise, though, the rest of the day passed in comfortable companionship. The earlier tension between them dissolved by Jack's concerted effort to keep the focus between them lighthearted and fun. Before lunch, they'd gone for a walk around the rocks and had even swum again in the giant rock pool without so much as a touch between them. Her awareness of him, however, increased with every minute that passed.

She found herself constantly looking for similarities and differences between the man he was now and the boy he'd been. There was a vein of steel running through him now, she recognised. A hardness about him that had never been there before. No doubt it had come about after his father had died and he'd stepped into his father's role as head of the household. Lily remembered Bradley Dolan as a quiet, gentle man. He'd been brilliant at his job, her father had often said so, but Charles's praise of Bradley Dolan had ceased when she and Jack had started going out. Her father had never fully approved and had gone to great lengths to prove the differences between them.

It had been a futile attempt to control a teenage girl. The harder he'd tried to push her away from Jack the stronger she'd held on. She'd sometimes wondered, if her father had condoned their relationship, whether it would have run its course and died a natural death. Once the forbidden became accepted, would they both have lost interest?

She knew she shouldn't have touched him so intimately but she couldn't help herself. Couldn't hold herself back. And that was how it had always been with her and Jack. She'd been helpless to say no.

Eight

It was late afternoon when they packed up their things and moved from the beach back to the boat. As Jack held the dinghy steady at the back of the boat she clambered aboard and then helped him to stow their things away before he pulled the dinghy up and secured it to the transom again.

"I thought we'd have fresh scallops for dinner before we head back. What do you reckon?"

"Really? That would be great. They're my favourite seafood."

"I remember." Jack gave her a smile that sent sizzling heat all the way to the pit of her belly.

Obviously that wasn't all he remembered. Lily thought back to the time they'd gone with masks and snorkels and gathered scallops off the sea bed near the beach where they lived. They'd opened them and barbecued them on the beach, before falling to their blanket and making love with wild abandon on the darkened shore.

"So are you up for it? There's a bed not far from here, it's not too deep so we won't need scuba. Snorkelling will be okay. Just like old times."

"I don't know about my stamina, but I'm prepared to give it a go," Lily answered.

"That's my girl."

He scaled the stairs to the flybridge and started up the motors before winching up the anchor. Once they were under way he gestured to her to take the wheel.

"Come on, have a go. You'll love it."

"Are you sure about that?"

"Sure, I'll be right behind you. You can drive a car, why not the boat?"

Lily stepped in front of him, feeling the hard, hot heat of his body down her back as she put her hands on the wheel. Jack leaned forward to murmur in her ear.

"Turn gently and get the feel of her. She's highly responsive so don't try anything too crazy."

She shivered, a sensation that had nothing to do with cold, as the warm air from his breath caressed her neck. After a while she began to relax, leaning back against him and following his commands as she steered the boat toward the scallop bed. She felt almost bereft when he pulled away from her when they reached their destination and anchored. She wanted nothing more than to turn and face him and press herself against his body and into his arms. To tell him she didn't want to take things slowly anymore. She turned, the words on her lips, but he was on the main deck already, a rear hatch open, and reaching inside for the snorkelling gear and a catch bag.

"Are you coming, or are you going to stay up there all day?" His teasing voice galvanised her into action.

She'd be totally and utterly foolish to give in to her feelings right now. Everything in her life was in a state of flux. To enter into a relationship that promised to be highly volatile would be emotional suicide.

By the time they'd gathered their quota and brought the shellfish on board, Lily was exhausted. Jack took one look at her and sent her below to shower and change while he prepared the shellfish. On the lower deck Lily used the guest bathroom. She took from her tote the change of clothes she'd packed, a light cotton sweater with elbow-length sleeves in the same cool blue as her eyes, and a pair of white jeans. After her shower, she lathered on moisturising lotion. Despite her care in the sun, the tops of her shoulders were a little pink and she didn't look forward to putting on her bra, no matter how fine and silky the fabric.

She wasn't the most heavily endowed woman and the top was finely woven enough to wear without a bra so Lily stuffed her bra back inside her bag and quickly pulled on her clothing. She slicked back her wet hair, in the warm evening it wouldn't take long to air dry and she knew after the sea bath it had had today that it would be a riot of soft curls as it dried. For once, the untamed and uncontrolled style suited her right down to the ground.

Lily gathered all her things together, made sure she hadn't left a mess in the compact bathroom, then went back upstairs. While she'd been showering Jack had obviously also been below decks to freshen up. His hair gleamed dark and wet against his scalp, and a fresh hint of cologne teased her nostrils as she joined him at the back of the boat. He'd dressed in a white polo shirt, which emphasised his tan, and a pair of well-worn denims hugged his hips and thighs.

He stood over a small gas barbecue, which shimmered with heat. As she got closer Jack drizzled some olive oil on the hot plate then tossed the freshly caught and shelled scallops on the surface.

"You amaze me," Lily said as she watched him, mesmerised by the play of muscles in his forearm as he flipped the spatula again.

"Amaze you? Why?"

"You're so capable. Is there anything you can't do? I mean, look a this." She swept her arm across to encompass the boat. "You have this boat, you have an amazing home, a successful business—and you cook!" She finished on a bright laugh.

"Reserve judgement on the cooking until you taste this lot." Jack smiled in return.

Jack scooped the scallops off the plate and shared them over two bowls of mesculun salad greens, then leaned over to pick up a small bowl in which Lily spied oil infused with finely chopped dill, which he poured lightly over the sea food. The aroma made Lily's mouth water. He finished off the meals with a twist of lemon pepper and handed Lily the bowls, gesturing to her to take a seat on the white leather banquette at the back of the boat. He'd put up a narrow wooden folding table, set side by side for the two of them, and a bottle of champagne settled on a bed of ice in a bucket with two champagne flutes beside it.

After he'd turned off the barbecue he lifted the bottle and poured off two glasses. Handing one to Lily, he raised his in a toast.

"To a great day."

Lily raised her glass to his and smiled. "Yes, a great day. Thank you." She took a sip of the wine and the liquid slid down her throat like nectar.

They settled at the table. Jack's leg brushed against hers, its solid presence a comfort and a torment. Only two layers of fabric separated them. Lily took another cooling sip of wine before lifting her fork, determined to distract herself from his proximity and her reaction to it. Her sensory neurons slipped into overdrive as she tasted a scallop. She couldn't stop the moan of sheer pleasure that evolved.

"God, this is so good. I'd forgotten how delicious fresh scallops could be." She lifted a napkin to her lips and dabbed at them, her hand suddenly arrested by the flare of heat in Jack's gaze as he watched her actions.

Instantly her body leaped to life, every cell attuned to the glow of passion in his eyes. Her breath hitched in her throat and an intense pull of longing centred deep within her womb. Her internal muscles contracted, sending a spasm of desire in a sharp pulse through her body. A tiny shudder rippled through her. If he reached for her now, just the merest touch, she feared she'd melt straight into his arms.

He was like a drug, intoxicating and addictive, and

somehow today he'd woven a cloak of need around her she'd been in denial of for years.

Lily forced herself to look away, to focus on her meal, but every morsel, every mouthful, only served to underline the fine wire of tension that bound them together. Her hand shook slightly as she took another sip of her wine and turned to watch the sun drift into the sea in a blazing orange ball of fire. The sky around them radiated colour—reds, pinks and oranges in varying hues—the clouds on the horizon kissed with a deep purple that faded into grey.

She wished she could capture this moment in time forever. Remain suspended in animation. Everything—the sensations that coursed through her body, the taste of the food on her tongue, the company she kept. A pang of loss struck deep at her core in the knowledge that such a dream was ephemeral. If she'd learned nothing else in the past ten years it was to take moments like this and lock them away to treasure them. Nothing stood still. Not joy. Not pain. Time marched on.

"It's beautiful, isn't it?" Lily commented on the innumerable colours marking the sky.

"Yeah, beautiful."

Something in the tone of Jack's voice forced Lily to turn her head to face him. He wasn't looking at the sunset, he was looking only at her.

He put down his wineglass and lifted the bottle to top her glass up again. She pressed her fingers on his arm when the glass was half full.

"No more, please."

"I can see you home tonight, Lily, or we could stay

aboard. The choice is yours." His voice vibrated across her senses, stroking her nerve endings, enticing her to agree.

"I need to take this slowly, Jack. You're overwhelming me. I feel like I'm losing control and I promised myself I wouldn't do that again." She felt his withdrawal. "It's not that I don't want to stay. I do. But I'd be doing us both a disservice if I didn't find a sense of me, of myself, before I get involved with anyone again. I'd just be in over my head again."

Jack stroked a forefinger across her cheekbone and down along her jawline before tapping it gently against her lips.

"Shh, there's no pressure, Lily. We agreed on the beach, yes? Just two old friends rediscovering each other. We have plenty of time to do that."

He cupped the back of her neck and leaned forward, placing a chaste kiss on her forehead that was in total contrast to the raging hormones that spun chaotically through Lily's body.

"C'mon. Let's sort these dishes out and we'll head back. You look like you've had enough for one day."

Lily hesitated a moment before following Jack to the galley. He'd accepted her plea to hold off so quickly, so easily. In the past he'd have cajoled her, secure in the knowledge she'd capitulate eventually, and more recently her companions were as likely to have sulked if she'd spurned their advances, no matter how tactfully she'd done so. She had no idea how to deal with it, with Jack, anymore. He constantly surprised her.

The journey back to the marina was all too short and it was dark as they drew into the berth. Jack leaped lightly to the jetty to tie off the boat's lines. When he came back aboard Lily found herself wishing she'd taken him up on his offer to stay out overnight. It seemed almost criminal to draw their day to an end.

"Can I help with taking anything off the boat? Towels, rubbish?" she offered, realising she was at the point of doing almost anything to prolong the moment where she'd head off on her own in her car.

"No, it's okay. I have a man who'll take care of all of that in the morning," Jack explained.

"You have a guy just to clean the boat? Isn't that a bit pretentious?" she teased.

Jack laughed. "No, he crews for me sometimes, when I take business associates out on the boat for a day's fishing or things like that."

"I see." Lily chewed her lower lip for a moment. The time had come to say good night. "Well, thanks again for a really neat day. I haven't enjoyed myself so much in ages."

"It was my pleasure."

Jack took a step toward her and Lily's body tightened in anticipation. She wasn't disappointed. She felt the flash of heat between their bodies as he came closer, then that glorious heat was pressed up against her. Her tote slipped unheeded to the deck as her arms wound around his neck and she lifted her face to his. Jack placed one hand at the small of her back, urging her body against him, the other reaching up, his fingers taking her chin and tilting it as he bent to kiss her.

She strained ever so slightly upward as he hesitated for the briefest moment, and then finally, mercifully, his lips were on hers. Lily sank against his hard strength, imprinting him against the soft lines of her body as his lips seared hers. She parted her lips, meeting his tongue halfway with her own and engaging him in a duel of seduction. She felt him shake slightly at the contact, the sensation giving her a sense of power. In comparison to their last kiss on the beach the other night, now she felt as though she had the upper hand.

To know she had the power to affect him physically, to make him tremble with her kiss, sent a surge of feminine supremacy through her psyche. Lily pulled her arms from his neck and hooked them around his waist, sliding her hands under his shirt and across the warm skin of his back. She felt goose bumps rise on his skin as she trailed her fingertips back and forth, tracing the lower line of his rib cage, relishing the feel of him, the texture of his skin, his warmth.

His lips were hard and demanding and she gave back with everything inside her—with everything she was and more. The feel of him impressed upon her, denuding her of memories of past lovers, filling her senses with only him.

Blood pulsed through her veins, she felt more alive, hungrier than ever before. And only Jack could assuage the hunger. His hand, which had held her jaw so softly, stroked a gentle line down her throat, across her breasts and down to her waistband. She felt the slight change in temperature as the night air caressed her bare skin before it was replaced with the heat of his palm as he skimmed across her belly, then up higher until his large hand cupped her breast, gently squeezing the aching flesh with a tenderness that sent a spear of longing from her chest all the way to her core.

She pressed her hips hard against him to assuage the longing that built with increasing demand at the apex of her thighs and heard him groan at the contact. His fingers pulled lightly at her nipple and an answering cry broke from her mouth only to be consumed by his as he deepened their kiss—their sounds, their taste, their breath mingling as one.

There was no thought in her head but for the moment, for the rightness of how it felt to be in Jack's arms. Time stood still, the past slid into a netherworld where it no longer had the power to influence the here and now. Here and now was made up solely of the knowing they fit together, belonged together.

Lily traced her tongue along Jack's top lip, before drawing it slowly into her mouth, sucking at its softness before repeating the motion with his lower one. That he allowed her to do so, that he didn't overpower her with his masculinity or ever-increasing demand, only served to make her feel more feminine, more precious, in his arms.

The hand Jack had at her back slid down her spine, cupping her buttocks through the lightweight denim of her jeans and drawing her more firmly into the cradle of his hips. He broke away from their kiss and leaned his forehead against hers, his breathing fast.

"Lily, if we don't stop now, I won't let you walk away tonight. You'd better go. But we will revisit this. Next Thursday. My place, six-thirty. Dinner."

There was a tremor in his voice that gave truth to his words. Lily nodded silently, pressed one last farewell to the corner of his grimly tightened lips, then turned to collect her tote bag and leave the boat.

On the dock she turned to look back at him. A shiver of desire rippled through her at the expression on his face. It was still there between them, that connection, but if anything it seemed bigger, stronger, than before. The knowledge both empowered and frightened her. If they took this further, would she ever be able to walk away whole again? Her earlier belief that she could get Jack out of her system had been foolishly optimistic. He was as firmly entrenched in her as DNA was a part of her makeup.

"Sleep well, Lily." His voice drifted across the pier.

She nodded in acknowledgement, lifted one hand in a brief wave, then headed for her car. Next Thursday was an age away. Could she stand to wait that long? With painful clarity Lily acknowledged she wanted to see Jack again with a craving that would take some work to relieve. His reaction to her gave her hope, a belief that maybe they could make this work this time. Their love for one another had been torn apart before and they'd both made mistakes as young adults, mistakes they wouldn't make again.

Was it possible that they had an honest chance to make a new relationship work between them? A warm glow of hope radiated from deep in the pit of her chest.

She hoped so.

Nine

Jack watched Lily get into her car and drive away. Every nerve on his body stood on full alert. Damn, he hadn't meant to let their embrace go so far. Desire had caught him in its coil, swift and sharp. He couldn't let this get out of hand. There was no way on this world that he was going to let the hard work and planning of the past ten years go merely for the sake of another toss in the sheets with Lily Fontaine.

His blood still pounded in his veins and he fought to rid himself of the feel of her in his arms, against his body, against the painfully hard erection she'd aroused in him. He went through the motions of securing the boat before jumping lightly to the jetty and making his way to his car. Sleep would be a long time coming tonight, he acknowledged. It would take more than a cold shower to soothe the ache in his body.

She'd felt so perfect in his arms. As if she belonged there. And he had to stop thinking like that right here, right now. They'd trod that road before. One belabouring foot after the other. And they'd fallen from the track in a conflagration that had caused irreparable damage. His father's life would never be restored. The child Jack and Lily had was lost to him forever. He fed the anger anew, anything to prevent himself from leaping into his car and chasing Lily's more sedate vehicle at the high speeds it was capable of and forcing her to stop, to accompany him home. To make love with her all night long with the pent-up passion of years of denial.

He'd had lovers, he was no saint, but he'd never felt that emotional link with another woman that he'd had with Lily. He'd identified early on that having that missing link was integral to his success. Any indication of it rearing its head was enough to send him in the other direction. Nothing and no one would get in his way. Especially not Lily.

He had to use this near-overwhelming desire for her to his advantage. He'd set out to woo her, and he would continue to do so. Shoring up his defences so he wasn't wooed in return was the kind of discipline that had brought him thus far in life and in business. It was time he reschooled himself on those skills—before Lily got so far under his skin again that he lost sight of his goal.

Saturday morning arrived bright and clear, another gorgeous golden day. Lily woke with a start, dawning realisation at how late it was in the morning propelling her out of bed and into the shower before heading down to the kitchen fuelled with an energy and vigour she hadn't enjoyed for a long time.

The remnants of her father's breakfast was in the sink. A coffee cup. Lily shook her head. At this rate, the man would have an ulcer on top of the high blood pressure she already suspected he suffered from. She walked down the hall to his study and knocked firmly on the closed door before opening it.

"Dad?" She stepped into the room, shocked at the chaotic mess of papers strewn everywhere, but even more shocked at her father's appearance. His face was an unhealthy grey, his thinning hair sticking in all directions. A glum expression pulled his lips down and made his cheeks more jowly than usual.

"Finally up, hey?" He got up from his chair and rubbed at his face. "Have a good day yesterday?"

"I had a great time, thanks, Dad." Lily avoided mentioning exactly who with and where. No point in upsetting him more than he already looked. "You look swamped here. How about I get you some breakfast? You should probably take a break."

Her father gave her a narrow-eyed look, then shook his head slightly. "No, I'll be fine. What have you got planned for today?"

Butterflies fluttered in her stomach. Could she tell her father about the idea she'd had on the beach for the quality second-hand clothing store? She wasn't sure if she wanted to run the idea past him before she had some figures on shop rental rates in town and had sourced more information about demand and the logistics of bringing second-hand clothing down from the United States to New Zealand. She made a mental note to contact the Onemata Drycleaner. If this plan took off the owner would become her new best friend. Lily took a deep breath and decided to keep her fledging idea to herself.

"I thought I'd go into town for the day, take a look around, maybe do some shopping," she said as breezily as she could.

"Women!" Charles snorted. "All the same. Give them some spare time and all they want to do is shop."

Lily smiled. She certainly hoped that was the case. She watched as her father settled back down at his desk.

"Get me a coffee, would you?" he demanded, his attention solidly back on his papers.

Lily closed the door quietly behind her. He'd already forgotten her existence. Seemed he'd been that way ever since she came home, with the exception of the lunch they'd shared. In some ways it was easier this way, but the child inside her missed the man who'd always been full of loud laughter and bluster. The one who'd dusted her knees when she'd fallen from her bike. Her mother had left them both when Lily was only four; she barely remembered her aside from a soft touch at night when she'd had a nightmare, the drift of a floral perfume. After she'd gone it was as if she'd never existed. Even at four years old Lily had understood that any mention of her mother was forbidden. Lily used to wonder what life would have been like with two parents, had looked at her friends' families, and especially Jack's family, with some envy. She'd wanted that for her baby. In the end it hadn't come down to what she wanted at all.

Lily swiftly made a fresh carafe of coffee and poured some into a thermos to take through to her father, as well as a steaming mugful. He probably hadn't noticed that she'd switched his regular brand for decaf. Mrs. Manson had protested that he'd complain but so far there'd been no ructions. Her father gave her a cursory smile of acknowledgement when she took the tray into his office.

After a light breakfast Lily headed into town. It was difficult to find a park on the main street, in the end she went round a few blocks and parked in a shady residential avenue. The walk was no hardship, the local council kept the footpaths and kerbsides in immaculate condition. Lily almost felt as if she'd been transplanted to a totally different, far more affluent, part of the world than that where she'd grown up. Onemata was definitely on a positive growth swing. She was hoping she'd be able to capitalise on it.

A short walk around town showed a few prospective stores she could consider. She'd made notes of the agencies handling the leasing arrangements and would call them early next week. For now, though, she decided to stop and enjoy a coffee outside on the pavement and watch the foot traffic in the area.

By the time Lily was onto her third coffee in her third cafe she was both wired and knew which empty store was her first choice for her new venture. Her heart thrilled at the idea of putting her idea into something tangible. She had so much to do, so many ideas to pull out of her mind and put onto paper. She was on a total high by the time she set down her cup and headed for where she'd parked her car.

As she walked with swift, clipped steps she almost bowled into another woman coming out of a shop. It only took a second for Lily to recognise her—Jack's mother.

"Mrs. Dolan, I'm sorry, I didn't see you there," Lily apologised.

Tania Dolan gave Lily a look that could shrivel fruit in a bowl. "An apology? From a Fontaine? I never thought I'd see the day."

The older woman pushed past her, her shoulder giving Lily a deliberate nudge.

"Hey, there's no need for that. I didn't mean to bump into you," Lily remonstrated.

"No, your sort never *mean* anything, do you? Not what you do, or what you say. Just stay away from my family," Tania spat. "Between you and your father, you've done enough damage."

Lily stood and watched as Tania Dolan stalked off, her grey-haired head bowed, tension in every line of her body. She'd looked older than the mid-fifties Lily knew her to be. Losing her husband had clearly taken its toll, but the bitterness in their brief exchange had left Lily shaken and had definitely taken the shine off her day.

It plagued at her during her journey home. Maybe her dad could shed some light on it. He was still in his office when Lily arrived home. She put together a tray of food, filled a jug with mineral water, and put it all out on the patio with a light gauze throw over the top and went to get him. To her surprise he willingly left the office to join her outside for the meal, and without too many disparaging remarks about the low-fat, high-fibre compilation Lily had put together, he ate through his portion and took seconds.

When they were finished he sat back in his chair and looked out to the water. For the first time since she'd arrived home he was starting to look more relaxed.

"Dad? Can I ask you something?" Lily ventured. The incident with Tania Dolan niggling like a grass seed in a sock.

"What is it? Not more money, I hope?" He laughed jovially at his own joke but his smile didn't quite reach his eyes. He wasn't kidding.

Lily gritted her teeth. "Not more money, not right now anyway, although I do need to talk to you about an idea I have later. It's Tania Dolan."

Charles stiffened in his chair and his face lost all signs of humour.

"What's the problem?" His voice grew hard and cold. "Is she causing you any trouble?"

"Not trouble exactly." Lily rubbed her forehead, starting to feel the onset of a headache. Probably the result of the overload of caffeine this morning. "She said something odd to me in town, acted as if she really hated me."

"What did she do?" Everything about her father's posture went on the defence, as if he was bristling for a fight.

"I wasn't looking where I was going and I bumped into her as she came out of a shop. I apologised and she all but rammed the apology straight back down my throat—said something about it being out of character for a Fontaine to apologise for anything. And that we never mean anything we do or say." Lily poured herself a glass of mineral water and took a sip, surprised to see her hand shake slightly. Mrs. Dolan's anger was still taking its toll. "What's she talking about, Dad? You and Mr. Dolan used to work together. He was your right-hand man. Why is she so bitter?"

"Some people can't take criticism. That's all. His work had been slipping. I had to let him go. About the time you went away, actually. She didn't like it, nor did her eldest boy. I told you to stay away from her son then and I told you again the other day. I know you've been spending more time with him. They're all trouble, Lily. I thought you'd learned your lesson the last time. They don't stand by their mistakes."

Lily flinched at his words; that he clearly thought she was one of those mistakes couldn't have been more clear. Charles pushed back his chair and went to go back inside.

"Thanks for lunch, but next time do something with a bit of meat in it. I need to get back to my papers, I'm just about sorted, then maybe you can tell me about this new idea of yours. Something to keep you occupied would be good. Keep you out of trouble and away from Jack Dolan."

Well, that firmly put her back in her place in his eyes, hadn't it, Lily thought in frustration. In his mind, she was, and always would be, his little girl. She sighed inwardly. Arguing it with him now would be futile. She opted for the illusion of compliance.

"Sure, Dad, whatever. Tell me, before you go, are things going well at FonCom?"

"Soon will be. Yes, soon will be. Things have been tight lately—a lot of competition in the industry at present. We've had to sharpen our pencils and watch things for a while. I'm expecting a big contract, end of next week. Everything will be fine then. Just fine."

Lily sensed an undercurrent of desperation in his voice that she hadn't noticed before, as if by saying things would be all right, affirming it out loud, would make it so. Did everything now hinge on just one contract? FonCom had always been an industry leader. Her father's considerable wealth had been built on its success. She'd been buoyed on the cushion of that wealth all her life. Her father had provided a very generous allowance for her since he'd sent her away and she'd taken vast satisfaction in spending every penny and asking for more. It had been her only control in a life that had spun off its axis when he'd confronted her about her pregnancy.

From the outset he'd been determined to break her and Jack up. And he had. Their relationship hadn't been strong enough to weather the wrath of Charles Fontaine in his prime. How he'd found out about their plan to run away together she never knew. Obviously his spy network was still very much in force.

When he'd arranged for her to be boarded with a family in Auckland, one of his close friends on whom he could rely for complete secrecy, she'd been watched all the time. Virtually a prisoner in a gilded cage. Just like now. She'd been foolish to give her father back control over her life again. Somehow she'd break free.

* * *

The strain of the week was beginning to take its toll on Lily by the time Thursday dawned. Her father had made an effort to spend more time at home with her, probably to ensure she didn't do anything he disapproved of, she thought cynically. He hadn't been encouraging about her second-hand clothing store idea, but had told her to put a proposal together for him to look at and he'd consider financing her if it looked good on paper. For the past several days that was what she'd done, only taking a break for her run along the beach each day.

She looked forward to seeing Jack tonight with an eagerness that almost frightened her. He'd been in her thoughts almost every minute of every day and some aspects of her proposal were taking longer than they ought to due to her inattention and propensity to drift off in a daydream every time she saw a large white power launch drifting past on the ocean. Did he have the same thoughts about the day they'd spent together? she wondered. Was he looking forward to tonight as much as she? Several times she'd lifted the telephone to call him, just to hear his voice, but had chickened out at the last minute. What if he'd changed his mind? What if he told her their date was off?

Darn, she was daydreaming again. Lily tried to force herself to concentrate on the spreadsheet she'd painstakingly filled in on the computer. Keyboard skills had never been her forte—hadn't really been necessary in her world. But she'd have to take a course or something if she was going to make a success of this idea. To minimise costs she'd have to prepare as much of the books as she could for an accountant. She entered data into a few more cells on the computer, a smile of delight breaking across her face when the calculations worked perfectly.

An hour later she was roused from her budgets and estimates by the chime of the doorbell. Mrs. Manson's ponderous steps echoed down the hall as she trudged along the tiles to the front door and her exclamation of surprise made Lily rise from her seat to see who was at the door.

"Flowers for you, Lily," the housekeeper said, with a puzzled look on her face. "An admirer?"

"I have no idea," Lily answered as she stepped forward to take the perfectly formed posy of yellow rosebuds from her.

"There's a card," the other woman pointed out.

Lily had no doubt that if Mrs. Manson saw who'd sent her the flowers she'd be on the phone to Charles Fontaine with the news. Seeing no reason to give her grist for her father's mill, Lily merely smiled at the housekeeper and turned away. She'd read the card in her room, in private.

"Well," Mrs. Manson huffed, clearly annoyed at being thwarted in her attempt to discover who'd sent the flowers, "someone's popular for Valentine's Day."

The sour note in the woman's voice didn't deter Lily from her need for privacy. Upstairs she closed her door firmly behind her. She put the flowers on her dressing table, her fingers lingering a moment on the perfectly formed petals before she lifted the card from its clip and slid the envelope open.

See you tonight, dress formal. —J

A thrill of excitement scorched through her veins and she felt a flush of heat on her cheeks.

Valentine's Day. Lily hadn't even made the connection. It had hardly been celebrated here in New Zealand before she'd gone away, but Jack had made an effort, that first year they'd gone out, to give her something special. She remembered it now. A posy of yellow rosebuds he'd stolen from the municipal gardens in the centre of town. She could still see the cheeky smile on his face when he'd presented them to her after school. It had been the weekend after that they'd made love the first time.

Liquid heat pooled low in her belly. What would it be like to make love with him again? They'd always set one another on fire and if their past two liaisons were anything to go by, the next time would be no different. That they would make love tonight, she was in no doubt. Not after last Friday. She paused for a moment, a flicker of unease in the pit of her belly. The trouble with fire is that someone usually got burned.

She tucked the card deep to the back of her underwear drawer. May as well make Mrs. Manson work for her information, she thought as she skipped lightly back down the stairs to her proposal.

Lily was in a flutter of nerves by the time she started to get ready for the evening. She'd chosen and discarded several outfits before finally settling on a red halter-neck dress. The halter was made of ribbons of silk and beads that hung down her back, swaying with her every movement as she walked. The soft fabric skimmed over her unfettered breasts and clung to her waist before flaring out over her hips and thighs, and falling to just above her knees. Silver sandals on her feet, silver and garnet drop earrings at her lobes, a jangle of silver bracelets on her wrist, a slick of sheer lip gloss, and she was done. She turned in front of the mirror slowly.

A knock at her bedroom door halted her in her perusal. Charles Fontaine stepped inside without waiting for her to answer. His eyes riveted straight onto the posy of rosebuds.

"You're seeing him again." He issued the statement with a flat, cold expression in his eyes.

"Yes, I am."

"I expressly told you not to. I protected you from Jack Dolan once, Lily. I won't do it again."

"I don't need protecting, Dad, not anymore and certainly not from Jack." Lily stiffened her spine. She would not allow him to intimidate her. "Dad, I'm twenty-eight years old. I make my own choices these days. I've been doing it for a while now, remember?"

Her father laughed, a mirthless, cynical bark that had nothing to do with humour. "Well, missy, those choices haven't exactly been a roaring success to date, have they? If you were so grown up, and all, you wouldn't be here now, would you? Just remember why you came back."

"Dad, I loved him once. I need to do this. I need to go."

"Pah! Love! The misguided hormones of pair of randy teenagers. Just remember who puts a roof over your head and food in your belly. Who's provided for you all these years, looked out for you. That's love." Charles sliced through the air with his hand. "He'll likely do no more than leave you pregnant with another Dolan bastard, and if he does, and you let him, don't think I'll be there to protect you again. There's only so much a father can do for his child. Something a Dolan would never understand. Never!"

"Dad! You can't say that. The Dolans are a close family," Lily protested, horrified at her father's tirade. She'd never seen him so upset. Not even that night he'd told her he knew the truth about her pregnancy and had coldly informed her of how things would happen next.

"Close?" Charles spit the word out as if it was a bitter pill on his tongue. "So close Bradley Dolan committed suicide rather than stand up like a man and protect his family? Don't give me any more of that rubbish."

"Suicide?" Lily sank to her bed on suddenly unsteady legs. "No. You're wrong."

"Yes, suicide. Like a coward he took his own life rather than look out for his family." Charles sat next to her on the bed and took her chin in his hand, forcing her to look at him. "Change your mind. Don't go, there's my girl."

He got up and left the room, not waiting for her response. Lily sat there for a while, motionless while her mind whirled. Jack's father had taken his own life. She couldn't believe it. The man she'd known was full of fun, a deep love for his family and an intense pride in his work. He'd never have done something like that.

But what if he had? That would explain Tania Dolan's unhappy demeanour, Jack's driven success, wouldn't it? Whatever the truth, it had no bearing on how she felt about Jack. She would see him tonight. If anything, in the two weeks she'd been back, she'd learned one very important lesson. The teenage love she'd had for Jack before was nothing compared to the feelings he aroused in her now as a woman. He wanted the past left in the past—so did she. Given the opportunity, Lily hoped they could make a new beginning.

She forced herself to her feet, gathered her car keys off the bedside cabinet and tucked a silver cobwebby shawl in the crook of her arm before heading down the stairs and to the internal door to the garage. She hit the auto garage-door opener and slid into her car while the massive roller door pulled up. A movement in the corner of her eyes arrested her as she inserted the car keys in the ignition.

Her father stood silhouetted in the doorway, dark fury clouding his face. She turned away and started her car, slid it into gear and drove out into the night—to Jack.

Ten

When he heard Lily's light footsteps on the stairs at the front of the house, Jack pulled open the front door to welcome her. He didn't care if she figured he'd been waiting for her. He had. Impatiently. As soon as she reached the doorway he pulled her into his arms and kissed her, capturing her lips with all the hunger he'd kept at bay in the past week, all the while hoping her torment at their lack of contact was as great as his own.

"Missed me?" he growled in Lily's ear as he lifted his lips from hers and nuzzled her neck. She smelled of jasmine and vanilla, an intriguing combination that hit his olfactory senses and zapped straight to his groin.

"Just a bit." She smiled back.

He narrowed his eyes and looked at her. She was

smiling but he could clearly see there was no pleasure in it.

"What is it? What's wrong?"

"Nothing. Really. Just a silly spat with my dad. Nothing to worry about."

Jack pressed his lips together in a grim line. Trust Charles Fontaine to find some insidious way to stamp his personality on their evening. Well, he'd make certain that Lily's thoughts were as far away from her father as possible. It was a task that both challenged and excited him.

"Good. Because I'd hate anything to upset your appetite tonight." *For anything,* he added silently, for he fully intended to seduce Lily into staying the night with him. Nothing would yank Fontaine's chain harder than knowing his precious daughter was sleeping in Jack Dolan's arms—again. This seduction had been planned with the precision of a military exercise. It had started with their day out on the boat, the tease and tantalisation of her senses, and continued with deliberately having no contact in the past week. The flowers today had been a subtle touch, the short message on the card another string to his seductive bow.

He hooked his arm around her waist and led her inside. When they were in the middle of the living room he took her hand and twirled her around, whistling a long, low, wolf whistle from pursed lips.

"You look delectable tonight, Miss Fontaine." He smiled and pulled her to him again, swaying her body gently to the music he'd chosen for precisely this moment. Their proximity sent his blood thrumming in his veins, her scent swirling around him as they turned about the floor.

"You don't look so bad yourself," she replied, a breathlessness to her voice that told him he'd hit the mark with his intentions. A spark in her eyes replaced the dull look of pain she'd arrived with. Yes, everything was going to plan. His courtship was like a dance—slow, slow, quick-quick, slow—and he was most definitely in the lead.

The song on the stereo ended, slipping into the next and for a while Jack simply allowed himself to enjoy the feel of her willing body against his. As the song changed again, he led her outside onto the deck where he'd placed two chairs to face the ocean, a smaller table between them with two wineglasses and a perfectly chilled Marlborough Chardonnay in an ice bucket between them. He lifted the bottle, wiped the dewy moisture from its base, then poured them each a glass.

He handed Lily her drink and lifted his in a toast. She met his gaze as she lifted hers in response.

"To a spectacular evening," he toasted, his voice deep and strong, imbued with promise.

Her lips parted and a tiny smile pulled the corners up slightly. She lowered her eyelids in a gentle sweep before opening them again, her blue eyes sending him a silent message of assent. "A spectacular evening," she echoed.

"Take a seat and tell me what you've been up to this week," he invited.

He'd had tabs on her all week, had heard about her visits to a couple of local Realtors and her enquiries about a couple of the empty shops in the shopping area of town. It would be interesting to hear what she had planned. Lily Fontaine had never dirtied her hands in her life, except for when she'd dirtied them on him, he remembered ruefully. The prospect of her actually setting up a business should be a joke, but he had a suspicion, from what he'd heard, that her idea had strong merit for a place like Onemata.

Her face became animated as she talked about how she'd come to her idea and how she'd been gathering information on the costs of actually setting up the business, overheads for the running, supply of stock, et cetera. Eventually the last of the shadows in her eyes disappeared. He was surprised at the detailed lengths she'd gone to in her quest for information and statistics, even going so far as to contact the local business association for information.

"It's a big step," Jack commented as he topped off her glass of wine again. "What made you decide to do something like this?"

"I've finally learned I can't let other people dictate my life anymore. For too long I've just let them, been happy to let them."

Jack watched as Lily leaned forward in her seat, staring out at the glistening ocean, at the birds working the school of fish jumping in the water a few hundred metres off shore.

"I need to grow up, Jack. I need to be in charge of my life. Even tonight, my father thought he could control me, stop me from coming to see you. You know, when I got here, all I could think about was being back in your arms, feeling safe. It's really no different to how

I was ten years ago. Him trying to rule my life, everything I said or did, and me running to you for comfort." She gave him a wry smile, "Well, not exactly comfort, not always. But you know what I mean."

"Yeah," Jack agreed. She'd been her father's puppet, even when it had come down to their child. The son or daughter he'd been doing his best to track down and had consistently hit one brick wall after the other. "I know what you mean. Sometimes you have to take a stand. Do what you know is right for you." Like he was doing.

Tomorrow Charles Fontaine would hear the news of the lost contract, would hear it and weep at the loss because the insider news was that FonCom was unsustainable without it. Jack would tighten the noose so tight that Fontaine would never wriggle out of it again. Would rue the day he'd ever heard the Dolan name. And so would Lily, eventually.

He turned their conversation to more general matters, filling the time until he'd planned to serve their meal. Their entrées they would take outside, here on the deck, then he'd decided the main course would be at the cosily set coffee table in the lounge. The formal dining table was too vast, too impersonal for what he had planned. Lily would literally be eating from his hands and, he hoped, she'd return the favour for him.

When Jack brought out the Onion Mumm entrée and dipping sauce, Lily exclaimed in delight.

"Oh-hh, I haven't tried one of these since I was in New Orleans on a photo shoot. Did you prepare it yourself?" She eagerly tore off a "petal" and dipped it in the sauce before lifting the morsel to her mouth and closing her eyes as she savoured the piquant sauce with the onion.

"I have to admit, no, I didn't prepare it myself. Even I know when to defer to the experts." Jack smiled and watched as she took another piece of the battered and deep-fried onion, the same expression of satisfaction crossing her face as she ate it. "There's a spot of sauce, just here," he said, and leaned over. With the tip of his index finger he lifted off the tiny pearl of sauce from the edge of her lip. She watched as he brought his finger to his mouth, opened his lips and licked the sauce away with the tip of his tongue.

Instantly her cheeks flushed with warmth and her eyes brightened in the way he knew so well. Blood pooled in his groin. Lily had always been a generous partner, even if initially they'd both lacked experience. Tonight was going to be worth the wait.

By the time they'd progressed indoors and he'd brought out the finger-food platter of crayfish, lemon-pepper-seasoned calamari and chilli-lime-marinated mussels together with vegetable crudités, he noticed Lily's wineglass was empty.

"Would you like another glass of wine with dinner, or are you driving tonight?" His question was loaded. If she accepted the wine, it would be acquiescence to a lot more than just another drink.

She tilted her head up to look at him from where she lounged on the floor pillows he'd scattered around the coffee table. In the middle of slipping off her sandals, the soft folds of her dress spread around her like water. He looked forward to undoing the tie at the nape of her neck, to slowly uncovering her skin and to laving it with the attention he craved to give. He waited for her reply, every nerve in his body poised.

"I wasn't planning on driving tonight. If that's okay with you, that is."

A lump settled in Jack's throat. He swallowed to get past the restriction. "Yeah, that's fine with me." *More than fine.*

"I—um, I didn't bring anything with me."

"It's okay, you won't need anything other than yourself. I've got everything covered," he promised.

Suddenly he couldn't wait to get through with dinner. To hell with the slow and sensuous seduction he'd planned. He wanted her right now. But he was a man used to waiting. After all, hadn't he waited ten years to wreak his revenge on Charles Fontaine? He could wait another hour or two for the pleasure of holding Lily in his arms, beneath his surging body with her long, slender legs wrapped around his waist. He almost groaned out loud. Instead he turned and went back to the kitchen and brought through a bottle of wine to the table.

Instead of sitting opposite Lily, he knelt down next to her and reached for a piece of juicy white crayfish flesh.

"Here," he said, offering it to her. "This should be eaten alone, so you can savour just how delicate the flavour is."

His fingers tingled as she opened her mouth, taking the delicacy with her teeth, her lips grazing against his fingertips. He watched as she slowly chewed the tender meat, a moan of pleasure escaping her mouth as the subtle taste sensations danced over her tongue.

"Oh gosh, that's so good. I haven't had plain boiled crayfish in forever. I forgot how the simple pleasures are often the best. Here, you try some."

She eagerly leaned forward and scooped some of the meat from one of the half shells on the platter and held it to Jack's lips. He hesitated a moment before taking her offering, his eyes locked on hers as he opened his mouth, sucking in her fingers with the piece of meat, stroking them with his tongue before letting her go. Her pupils flared in reaction to the intimate sensation of his tongue, her lips parted, her tongue at the edge of her teeth.

"Yeah, simple pleasures," Jack said, his voice deep. "The best."

Lily burned with anticipation. For each selection of food Jack offered, a coil deep inside her tightened up a notch. His closeness, the scent of him, the sheer heat that radiated from his body, sent her mind into overdrive. Was he as aroused as she at the moment? Did his entire body thrum with the rhythm of their breathing? With the tease and dance of feeding one another with the exquisite flavours, sating the olfactory senses yet stirring up a physical hunger that built and built like a bonfire of need?

She'd never found eating a meal to be such a sensory pleasure before, but tonight it was as if every sense in her body was magnified, strengthened by the seduction of her taste buds and by the promise of what lay ahead. A flutter of nerves skittered down her spine. She'd been certain in her mind she was ready to take this next step with Jack, but now as the time drew nearer, she felt as skittish as if they'd never been intimate, as if she had no idea of what type of touch drove him to distraction or the look in his eyes in the seconds before he climaxed.

She shivered as a pull of longing drew through her body and the coil of tension in the pit of her belly tightened up another notch. All of a sudden she couldn't wait to get her hands on him. She wanted gratification, hard and fast, and she wanted to give it, too.

They'd almost completed the seafood platter, the taste sensations lingered on her tongue, but she wanted a different flavour now. She wanted him.

"Jack?" She trailed her hand up one of his strong forearms, the dusting of masculine hair tickling her fingers.

"Hmm?"

"Is there dessert?" She smiled at the surprise on his face.

"Yes. Are you ready for dessert?" His voice was cautious, testing.

"I'm ready. Very ready. But not for dessert. For you."

Lily rose up onto her knees and straddled Jack's hips, his long legs trapped under the table in front of him. She rocked her pelvis against the hard line of arousal she felt beneath her and bent her head to take his lips in a kiss with which she wanted to demonstrate just how much she wanted him.

His lips were slightly glossy with the juice of the marinated mussels, the tang of chilli and lime initially overwhelming his own intrinsic flavour. She deepened the kiss, sweeping her tongue into his mouth, swallowing his groan of need, pressing her heated core more firmly into his groin. She felt him shudder beneath her. With another groan, Jack pulled away from her. He shoved his hands up into her hair, holding her head still and forcing her to meet his simmering amber stare.

"Tell me you're not going to change your mind, Lily. At this point I could just about let you go, but trust me on this, in another second I won't be capable."

She smiled. A soft secret smile as old as the attraction between the sexes.

"I'm not leaving you tonight, Jack. I want you. More than I've ever wanted you or anything else. Let me show you."

She took his lips again, felt his fingers bunch and tighten almost painfully in her hair before they cupped the back of her head, drawing her in closer as if he, also, couldn't get enough of her. Incredibly, she felt his erection grow even harder and she rocked against its length, feeling the dampness grow at the apex of her thighs. She was so ready for him now she shook with the wanting. Already she hovered on the brink of orgasm. No other man had ever had this incendiary effect on her. She'd never loved another as she loved Jack Dolan.

A spear of shock plunged through her. Love? How had that happened so quickly? But deep inside Lily acknowledged that it hadn't been a quick transition. The feeling in her heart had dwelled there dormant, suppressed for ten lonely years while she struggled to find what was missing in her life. And all along it had been here. At home. With Jack.

She felt his hands tugging at the ties of her halter, his fingers trembled in their haste. She took her mouth from his and straightened slightly, and lifted her hands to assist him, deftly undoing the knot of ribbons and beads.

His hands dropped away as she caught up the ends of the fabric then slowly lowered them, exposing first the gentle swell of her breasts then her taut nipples, darkened and questing for his touch, before she dropped the fabric away completely. It pooled around her waist in a carmine swirl, the jewelled colour of the fabric a strong contrast to her lightly tanned skin.

Shivers of delight chased up her skin as Jack's hands wrapped around her slender waist then skimmed upward, feathering over her rib cage before tracing a fine line under her breasts.

"Ah, it's still there," he said, satisfaction ringing in his voice.

"What?" she asked, her voice heavy with desire.

"Your birthmark."

He leaned forward and his tongue traced around the heart-shaped birthmark she'd all but forgotten about. Jack teased her with tiny licks across the surface of her breast until she all but begged him to take her nipple into the hot, wet cavern of his mouth.

Despite her pleas he appeared in no hurry and Lily felt as if her skin would split with the tight demanding need that rose within her, the pressure building and building, seeking release yet not finding it.

His fingers continued their feather-fine tracery of the underside of her breasts as he paid due homage to her birthmark. Finally his tongue traced a track from the underside of her breast and up toward her engorged nipple. Again he teased, swirling his tongue around but not over the tight bead of flesh. Lily rocked her hips harder, physically begging him to take her nipple in his mouth.

When his lips closed over the tightly ruched skin, Lily nearly jolted off his lap. A spear of sharp building sensation arrowed down through her belly to her inner core. She felt the contractions begin in her womb as his tongue played across her nipple, drawing it into his mouth, releasing it and then starting all over again. His other hand slid down her body, seeking, questing beneath the gathered fabric of her skirt. His fingers traced a new feather-soft line from behind her knee and up to her buttocks where he cupped the warm globe of flesh, exposed by her G-string, in his hand. He squeezed slightly, pulling her ever more firmly against him. A shudder started from deep inside her, her nerve endings screamed for release.

His hand slid across her hip, to the hollow at the top of her thigh, his fingers slipping inside the tiny triangle of fabric now soaked with the juices from her body. Lily angled her hips slightly upward, allowing him better access to the aching nubbin, the centre of all her pent-up need. He barely touched her, once, twice, a gentle sweep of his finger, and she came apart in his arms, his name a savage cry from her throat as paroxysms of pleasure rode through her body in wave after wave.

Eventually she sagged against him, her head nestled against the curve of his neck and his shoulder. Her heart beat so fast, so loud, it almost felt as though it would leap from her chest. Slowly her breathing returned to normal, but the aftershocks of her orgasm continued to send little shocks of pleasure through her body, leaving her feeling boneless, helpless in his arms.

"You cheated," she murmured against his throat,

nipping lightly at his skin. "You made me come but took no pleasure for yourself. This time is for you."

"Don't kid yourself, Lily." His voice was rough like gravel, as if each word was being ripped from his throat. "I take the utmost pleasure in watching you lose control, in feeling you fracture apart in my arms, knowing I brought you that pleasure."

"Then you'll understand my need to reciprocate."

Lily pushed against his shoulders, using his solid strength for balance as she regained her somewhat shaky composure and slowly stood over him. She pushed at the dress, bunched around her waist, letting it slid down over her hips before it fell to her feet. One by one, she lifted her feet, stepping out of the pool of fabric, then she flicked it away with a gentle kick. Still standing over Jack's prone body, she arched her back and stretched, like a cat in the sunshine. Sleek and proud and incredibly female.

"Lie down on the pillows," she commanded from her vantage point. "It's your turn."

Eleven

Jack silently did as she bade, all the while not taking his eyes from her body. Lily's breasts felt full and tight, her skin ultrasensitive, as if with his gaze he physically touched her.

When he was positioned against the pillows she knelt beside him, her fingers flying over the black studs of his shirt, inch by inch exposing the broad expanse of his chest to her touch. She pushed the fabric aside with impatient movements, her palms skimming over his skin, leaving a trail of goose bumps in their wake. She ran her hands across the tops of his shoulders and down across his pectoral muscles, which twitched beneath her touch. The hard disks of his nipples abraded her hands as she swept them across his skin.

Slowly she worked her way down his body, pulling

the tails of his shirt from his trousers and loosening the belt at his waist. Ever so carefully she eased down the zipper, mindful of the tender swollen flesh that pressed against it. He lifted his hips as she pushed his pants down, a raw groan pulled from his throat as her fingers traced the outline of his erection through his boxers. She felt his penis jump against her hand as she rubbed against him more firmly before she eased his boxers down, exposing the hard length of him to her gaze, her touch, her taste.

She bent and swirled her tongue around his tip, the tangy, salty taste of him exploding on her tongue as she swept away the bead of moisture that glistened there. Again and again she circled the engorged head, her fingers wrapped around his shaft and pulling slowly, rhythmically, along is length. She bent lower, her hair tickling against the paler skin at the top of his thighs, his groin, and took his tip into her mouth, her lips slickly closing around him, sliding over the silken hot flesh with a new hunger.

Her own body began to throb anew with the beat of heated blood as it pulsed through her. With her free hand she cupped his swollen sac, squeezing gently, and sucking with increasing pressure on his sensitive skin at the same time.

Jack's hands, which had remained still at his sides while she ministered to him, suddenly whipped up and clenched in her hair, holding her to him as she continued to swirl and suckle and squeeze. She felt the tremor build within him, felt the muscles of his stomach, his thighs, clench—half lifting off the bed of pillows—as his climax exploded through him.

With a satisfied smile she lifted her head from him, stroking his length one more time as she stretched out alongside his body, trailing her fingers up across his belly and higher to rest flat across his heart—over the tattoo of a lily he'd never had removed.

They lay in silence for some time, the golden light from the setting sun gilding their bodies. Lily had never felt more powerful or complete at the same time. They hadn't even fully made love yet and still the sense of satisfaction, of completion, that coursed through her veins knew no par. She had brought him the utmost pleasure, and it pleasured her to know she'd done so. Pleasured, empowered and aroused.

She wanted him again. All the way this time. More than just a touch, a mouth at her wildly sensitive breasts. She wanted—no, she *needed* to feel his heavy weight over her body, his total possession of her.

Jack stroked a lazy hand up and down Lily's spine. He wanted to feel her skin against his and he was wearing far too many clothes. He pulled away from her, and levered himself to his feet and rearranged his boxers and trousers before reaching down to pull Lily to a standing position.

"Now that's got the edge off, you'd better be ready for round two," he growled as he scooped up their wine bottle and their glasses from the table. "Here, take these."

Lily took them and laughed in surprise as he scooped her up into his arms as if she weighed no more than a child. He bent and nuzzled her breast, catching her nipple in his teeth and pulling gently.

"You seem to have an obsession with my breasts, Mr.

Dolan," Lily teased with a soft chuckle that ended on a moan as he did it again.

"Your breasts and every other part of you, Miss Fontaine."

He ascended the stairs with her in his arms, stopping on the landing to kiss her deeply. "All night long, Lily. I'm going to drive you wild, all night long."

"You'd better deliver on that. I'm counting on it."

He covered the rest of the stairs at a jog, wheeling to the left at the top and through another sitting room before entering the master bedroom. There, he lowered Lily to her feet, deliberately sliding her down over his body. He was already hard for her again. He took the wine and glasses from her and placed them on the bedside cabinet before shedding his clothes and reaching for her again.

A shudder ran through his body as the tips of her nipples brushed against his chest and he ran his hands down her back before sliding his fingers under the thin strip of her G-string and pushing it down off her. His erection pressed against her entrance, demanding entry as if it had a life of its own. But he pulled back, summoning on all of his control, and led Lily over to the bed. He ripped away the covers and gently pushed her down onto the cool, crisp, cotton sheets, his eyes drinking in her grace as she lay there, a secret smile tilting her lips.

He hoped she had enough stamina for what he had in mind because now he had her here, in his house, in his bed, he wasn't letting her go for a very long time. Before he joined her on the bed he yanked open the bedside drawer and scooped up a handful of condoms, scattering them on the polished surface of the wood.

"So many?" Lily said with a smile.

"I have more," he grunted as he ripped one of the packets open and sheathed himself with an economy of movement before positioning himself over her. "This one is going to be wild, I hope you're ready for me."

He reached between her legs; a swell of pride coursed through him when he found she was slick with desire for him already. She lifted her hips to him in silent entreaty as he positioned himself at her entrance. Jack reached for her hands, pinning them back against the pillows, opening her body to him fully.

Her small breasts jutted forward, her back slightly arched, and he watched the flush of arousal creep across her throat and bloom over her chest as he slowly inched himself inside her. Her muscles clenched around him and he waited until they eased off before surging into her, burying himself to the hilt, his sac brushing against her skin. He pulled back and surged forward again, this time, impossibly, even deeper than before. Her eyes glazed with passion, her breath gasped from her swollen lips. Again and again he plunged, riding her thrusting hips with a hunger that built and built within him until he poised on the pinnacle of his pleasure.

Lily writhed against him as he hesitated. A couple more strokes and he'd be over the edge, and he wanted her over that edge with him, screaming with gratification.

"Are you with me, Lily?" He ground out the words.

"Oh God, yes. Please. Don't stop now."

Her inner muscles clenched around him again, pulling him deeper into her body and he sank into her, once, twice, three times, losing himself in the starburst of bliss that exploded through him and in the cries of completion that fractured from Lily's throat.

It was a while before coherent thought returned to him. He withdrew from Lily, her small moan of protest making him smile.

"I'll be back," he promised with a swift kiss on her naked shoulder.

In the en suite bathroom he dispensed with the condom. It went against his plan to be using any form of contraception, but for some reason he couldn't bring himself to deliberately tamper with the things. One way or another, he would impregnate Lily Fontaine. She'd bear for him the child she owed him, and he'd have the ultimate satisfaction of letting Charles Fontaine know it.

He wondered if Fontaine was waiting up for Lily's return home tonight. Well, the old man would have a long wait on his hands. Jack wasn't anywhere near finished with her yet. Not by a long shot.

It was almost dawn when Lily woke. Her body felt used and tender, but deliciously so. A satisfied smile crept across her face. Jack had been insatiable, and she'd loved every second of it. Eventually they'd had their dessert—here in bed, the white-chocolate mousse a form of foreplay in itself—and they'd shared the last of the wine from one glass. The sense of togetherness had felt so right.

She stretched against the fine cotton of the bedsheets with a sigh of deep contentment and looked across to where Jack lay sprawled on the other side of the bed. The pale sheets showed up his dark tan, even in the half light.

Carefully, so as not to disturb him, she slid from the bed, grabbing up the feather-light duvet that had slipped to the floor during the night and wrapping it sarong-style around her. A set of bifold wood-and-glass doors led off the master suite to a private balcony. Lily eased the door open and slipped through, grateful that the door hadn't made any noise. She curled up on one of the sun loungers, positioned to face the ocean, and watched the sun as it slowly began its traverse into the sky. The myriad colours reflected on the bank of clouds at the horizon—pink through to peach and varying tones of lilac and red—bespoke imminent rain. She hoped it would be a squally summer storm that lashed the beach and threw driftwood high up onto the sand. There was nothing quite as exhilarating as a summer storm.

"Can't sleep?"

Jack's deep voice made her start. Lily turned to face him, her breath catching in her throat at the magnificent picture he made standing there, powerful and naked, and bathed in the glory of the sunrise.

"Hmm," she agreed. "Besides, it's a long time since I've seen an Onemata sunrise."

"Is there room under that duvet for the both of us?" he asked.

"Sure." Lily rose from the lounger and spread the duvet out over the cushions. "Here, you sit down first, I'll climb on your lap."

Jack did as she suggested, and once she was settled he scooped up the edges of the duvet and wrapped them around them both. Lily sighed in contentment. There was something very special about being wrapped in the arms of the man she loved and quietly watching the beauty of the day unfold before them. Although she could feel he was semi-hard, he seemed content to simply hold her. This was how she'd always imagined they'd be. Together. A couple. They'd missed out on so much. And why? Her father's interference aside, Jack wasn't the kind of guy who'd just give up. She had to know what had made him give up on them.

"Jack, can I ask you a question?" she asked.

"Uh-huh." He nuzzled at the back of her neck, sending a shiver of goose bumps down her spine and making her squirm slightly against his lap.

"I'm serious. I need to know something."

"What is it?"

"What went so wrong with us ten years ago? We had so many dreams, so many plans. But we didn't do any of it, did we? I never finished uni, you stayed here in Onemata. How did we get so off track?"

"Your father made sure we did." Jack's answer was short and laced with bitterness.

"Dad?"

"You think you know what he's capable of, but seriously, Lily, you have no idea. You know how we'd waited until you received your course acceptance for Auckland University and how we'd planned to move up there together?"

"How could I forget."

He pressed a kiss into the curve of her neck. "Yeah, well a couple of weeks before we were due to leave, your father called me into FonCom. He told me to leave you alone, that I was holding you back and that you'd never amount to anything with me in your life."

Lily held her breath. Waiting, wondering. Would he tell the truth about the money her father had paid him to stay away from her?

"He threatened me, Lily. But I didn't believe him. Didn't believe he'd go through with it." Jack's voice shook slightly, as if the memory still had the capacity to shock him.

"What did he do? Tell me, Jack. What was it?"

At the time she couldn't believe her father had discovered their plan to leave Onemata together. They'd been so careful to ensure that no one knew, not even their friends. Jack had been working and saving for months so they could find a small flat or apartment of their own. Where they could set up house together while they both pursued their degrees—his in business administration, hers in the arts.

"He told me that if I didn't back off, he'd fire my dad from his job. He was prepared to sack the person who'd been his right-hand man and his senior design engineer since he set FonCom up.

"Dad was expecting to be offered a partnership, Lily. It would have set him up for life and it was something he'd worked toward—something your father had promised him—for years. He gave everything he had to FonCom because he believed in your father's vision for the firm and his ability to push the company onto the global stage. But the company only reached that level of success because of Dad's software design skills.

"I didn't believe that your father would do such a

thing. That he'd cut off his nose to spite his face by firing Dad. I told him I wouldn't leave you for anything or anyone. I told him we were in love and that I wanted to marry you, but he just laughed in my face. He said a Dolan would never be good enough for his daughter. He made it clear that whatever happened next would be on my head, and mine alone."

There was an element in Jack's voice that rang painfully true. She'd heard similar words often enough from her father. A finger of doubt traced the back of her mind. Had her father lied to her all along about paying Jack to stay away? She'd been so distraught, so displaced, she'd believed him. Especially when Jack hadn't returned her frantic call when she'd arrived in Auckland.

Lily turned in Jack's arms. "You never said anything of this to me! Why didn't you tell me. I could've—"

"You couldn't have done anything. No one could. I still didn't believe him. I tried to talk to my father about it, but he was so busy ironing out the bugs in that programme they sold to the International Banking Commission that we never got the chance."

Jack sighed deeply. "The day we were supposed to leave, your father delivered on his threat to me. He fired my dad from the job he loved."

"That's awful, Jack, but your father was highly skilled. Surely he could've got another job somewhere else?"

"There's more," Jack said in a voice filled with acrimony. "I was so angry I went up to FonCom and demanded to see your father, insisted that he give my dad his job back. I can still see the smug look on his face now. He told me that Dad could have his job, but only if I stayed away from you—if I didn't, he would invoke a restraint clause in Dad's employment contract preventing him from working within the software industry for three years." Jack paused and took a deep breath before continuing. "You have to understand, Lily, Dad's work was his life. He truly loved what he did. To be told he wouldn't work in the industry again for three years, well, it was like being told he'd never work in the industry again. It's fast-moving, subject to change and innovation on a regular basis. He couldn't afford to be out of it for so long, but he couldn't afford not to work, either."

"I wish I'd known. I could have appealed to Dad, begged him to do something, anything, to give your dad his job."

Lily's voice shook with emotion. As awful as it was, she knew her father was capable of such perfidy. He had always been driven and it had always been his way or no way at all. Neither of them had stood a chance against him, as young as they were.

"It wouldn't have made any difference. Charles Fontaine is an immovable object when he's made up his mind. You know that. I went home from that meeting feeling utterly helpless. I told my parents what your father had said. My mother begged me to stay away from you, but I couldn't. When I got to the old weigh station, where we'd agreed to meet, your father was waiting for me. He took one look at me, shook his head with that cynical smile he wears, and got in his car. Before he drove away he told me that I was pathetic and that he was glad you'd finally seen the light. He said you'd already gone to Auckland and that you never wanted to see me again.

"I felt sick to the soles of my feet when I saw that look on his face. Sick and torn apart. I had no idea where you were. I raced home, called your place, but there was no answer. You'd gone."

"He'd sent me away, Jack. I had no choice."

Her father had stormed home from work early in an absolute rage and had told her he knew about her pregnancy. He'd been disgusted with her and at eighteen she hadn't stood a chance against his ire. Within the hour he'd arranged for her to be in a car with a driver and had transported her to stay with a family in Auckland she'd never met before. People who'd owed her father a favour. It must have been a big one because while they looked after her physically, she'd been nothing more than a captive to her father's demands.

She stroked her fingers down his cheek, across his firmly pressed lips. "I called you when I got to Auckland and left a message begging you to come and get me, but when you never called back, I gave up. Dad had told me not to expect anything from you, had said you wouldn't be there for me when the chips were down. I thought he was right. I had no idea of what he'd done to your family."

Jack blew out a sharp breath.

"I couldn't come because when I got home that night Dad had taken the car and gone out. Mum was beside herself. She said Dad had told her he was going to talk to Fontaine, that one way or another he'd make sure we were all provided for. He was so upset, she was terrified he would do something stupid. I took off on the bike, looking everywhere. Eventually, I found his car wreck on the road leading back to town from your place, wrapped around a power pole."

"Oh, God, no! Was he..." Lily couldn't bring herself to say the word *dead.* She couldn't imagine what Jack must have gone through.

"He died just after I found him. He apologised to me Lily. Apologised, for chrissake! He'd done nothing wrong. He'd worked hard all his life to support his family and yet your father still made him feel as if he had to apologise."

Lily felt the anger emanating off Jack in waves. Anger tinged with unassailable grief. She felt helpless in the face of his despair, incapable of offering him solace.

"You know what made it worse, Lily? Your father gave evidence at the inquest as to Dad's state of mind. You see, Dad had gone to him, begged him for another chance, and Fontaine had refused. The coroner ruled suicide, which meant that the insurance company wouldn't pay out on his life policy. It was left to me to provide for them. Finn had just started uni, Saffy and Jasmine were still at school and Mum was in no state to find work. I couldn't leave them and go searching for you. I had to stay and face my responsibilities. When you never called me again, I decided that I'd been no more than an adventure to you. A 'walk on the wild side' as all your friends had always said."

His comment on the day she'd arrived back made perfect sense now, she realised.

"No, you were never just a walk on the wild side, Jack. I loved you then." She reached up to kiss him. "I love you now."

Twelve

Jack stiffened in shock at her words. *She loved him?* The bitter irony of it swept through him like a tidal wave. As if love would make it all right, as if it could wipe the slate clean again. No. There was no way on this world that he wouldn't achieve the satisfaction and the result he wanted. Love meant nothing.

If she'd loved him she'd have told him about the baby. She'd have given him the chance, however small, to move heaven and earth to be a part of his child's life. She didn't know the meaning of the word. But she would know what it felt like to lose everything she held dear, as he had.

He kissed her again, tasting her, imprinting his own flavour on her. He pushed off the duvet that had cocooned them and lifted her from her supine position in his arms, turning her to face him. Understanding his intention, she positioned herself over him, running her soft, small hands over his shoulders, down his arms and back up again. She traced firm flat-palmed circles over his chest, her touch leaving a prickle of sensation where her hands had been.

He cupped her hips with his hands, tilting them forward, rubbing her hot, moist entrance across the base of his erection. She moaned and he felt her heat increase. She was haloed by the rising sun, the moisture at the juncture of her thighs now glistening gold in its rays. She took up the rhythm herself, rubbing along his shaft, back and forth.

Sensation spiralled through his body, pushing back the grief that had settled over him like a mantle of darkness while he'd told Lily about the night his father had died, pushing back the anger that filled him anew.

He could only focus on one thing. Lily. Her eyes were bright with passion, the pupils dilated. Her lips parted slightly, her tongue caught between her teeth as she continued, back and forth, back and forth.

She leaned forward and bit lightly at his nipples, then laved them with her tongue. First one, then the other. He'd never known such sensitivity. His erection grew painfully hard, jutting proudly from his body now that she had elevated herself slightly, her slick folds hovering tantalisingly just above him.

Her hands rested on his shoulders, bearing her weight against his strength. She lifted her face to kiss him again, pulling at his lips, his tongue, dragging a groan of need from deep inside of him. He wanted her with a hunger that came out of loss, a hunger that had been gnawing at him for ten long arid years. Years of focus, years of denial and sacrifice. He couldn't bear it any longer. Protection be damned. He had to be inside her. He pulled her down until the blunt head of his erection probed at her entrance. He hesitated, making eye contact with her, then thrust upward.

She shook all over as he entered her body, sinking down, taking him deeper inside, tilting her hips so she could accommodate him fully.

Jack clenched his teeth against the urge to pump his hips, to take from her the climax his body so desperately craved. No, he wanted her to do this. She had to take control. If she didn't stop right now, she would be the one responsible for driving their unprotected union to its conclusion—to any consequences that arose.

And then, mercifully, she began to move. Slowly at first, then increasing her tempo. She lifted her hands from his shoulders and cupped her breasts, offering them to him as she kneaded and squeezed at the perfectly formed mounds. Jack's hands slid up to her waist, holding her as he bent upward, taking one nipple in his mouth and pulling at the distended peak to the same beat as her hips pounded against his.

He saw the flush of orgasm creep across her skin, felt the exquisite tightening of her inner muscles as the ripples spread from her centre and out across her body. He grabbed her hips again as her body slumped against his, pumping hard as he burst through the barrier that held him earthbound and catapulted him into the dawn.

His breathing was ragged, his body slicked with perspiration, as was hers. He trailed his hand up and down her spine, lingering at the cleft of her buttocks before moving back upward again. He felt the aftershocks zap through her body, milking him of the last of his climax, prolonging the piercing satisfaction of his release.

Lily's heart beat hard against the wall of her chest, marching in time with his own. The cool morning air sent a shiver across his skin, like a finger of foreboding. Jack pulled the edges of the duvet back over them both and held her to him, his arms a band of strength around her. He forced away the feeling of belonging, of fulfilment, that Lily gave him so unreservedly—resolutely pushing to the furthest reaches of his mind, the craving she'd set up in him for more.

He would hold her to him for as long as necessary, he promised silently. Then he would unleash his revenge. A sharp pain hit him in the region of his heart, but he refused to allow it time to bloom into thought or reason. Nothing could interfere with his purpose. Nothing.

Lily drove home later that morning, her mind in turmoil. She should have told Jack about the baby. He deserved to know now, and he'd certainly deserved to know back then when she'd been bundled away by her father like so much unwanted baggage. She'd been too young to battle her father's wishes on her own. Certainly far too young to fight against the virtual internment she endured, wrapped in despair and a growing fear for her future and the future of her child. In the end it had all been for nothing. An undetected true knot in the baby's umbilical cord, an extended labour and her precious boy had been born dead. Telling Jack would have been unbearably cruel on top of what he'd relived telling about his father's death.

Lily rounded the bend in the road where Bradley Dolan had died; a cold frisson ran down her spine. How could her father have been so manipulative, so cruel? The ramifications of his actions continued to ripple through both families even now, ten years later. She steered her car into the long driveway that led to her father's beach home.

He'd worked all his life to provide her with everything a girl could want. Everything except the unadulterated love and acceptance of a parent. Everything except the encouragement to seek that from another in the natural continuum of life. She had to face him and find out the truth.

Charles's car was in the garage and Lily fought the sick feeling at the pit of her stomach. He was waiting for her. Goodness only knew what kind of mood he'd be in. It wasn't long before she found out. She'd no sooner left the garage when he bellowed her name. She stopped midstride, took a deep, levelling breath and went toward his office.

"You wanted to see me?" Lily kept her voice as cool as possible, inside she was quaking.

"You had to go and do it, didn't you?" Her father's voice seethed with fury.

"Do what, exactly, Dad?"

"You know what I mean. Christ, I can even smell him on you! You're as stupid now about that man as you were ten years ago. Next thing you'll be pregnant again. You don't know what the hell you're doing."

All warmth drained from her body as she stood up to her father's verbal assault. Far better to let him rant than to give him any further ammunition. His last comment, however, sent a chill through her. She *could* be pregnant again. The last time they'd made love they hadn't used any protection. The very act itself had been in direct response to Jack's emotional outpouring. It had pulled at every instinct in Lily's mind and soul to offer him comfort in the only way she knew how. The potential consequences had been the furthest thing from her mind. She should have known better. They both should have. But their lovemaking had been so perfect, so necessary.

"Stop it!" she cried, determined not to allow her father to sully what she and Jack had shared. "I know precisely what I'm doing. I'm taking my life back—*my life*. The life you stole from me. The life I chose. I love Jack, and that's not going to stop just because you throw your money and your weight around."

She took a deep breath and chose her next words carefully.

"I know what you did to the Dolan family. Whether you deny it or not, you're responsible for Bradley Dolan's death. How can you even sleep at night with that on your conscience?" She paused, ten long years of bitterness and frustration building to a head inside her. "Oh, that's right. I forgot. You don't have a conscience. People are just pawns to you, aren't they? Necessary vices to be tolerated until they've served their purpose. All you're interested in is money and the prestige it brings you."

Charles Fontaine went grey at her words, his mouth twisted in an ugly line. "It didn't seem to bother you to reap the benefits of that money or prestige. What do you think supported you over the years? Do you really think that talent scout just happened to come along at just the right moment in your life? Stop being so naive, Lily. I'm a powerful man, and I'm not averse to using that power to give me and mine what's due—and you're mine, Lily. No matter what you think.

"If I hadn't been so ruthless, you'd have had nothing. You'd *be* nothing. I did it all for you. Think on that the next time you want to open your legs for Jack Dolan. And while you're at it, ask yourself why he's sleeping with you again. This isn't about you anymore, my girl. It's about me."

He slammed his briefcase shut and stormed from the house. Lily stood still in shock as she heard the garage door open and his car rev to start. The stench of burning rubber filtered through the house as he spun the wheels of his car.

Eventually she gathered herself together and went up to her room where she slid out of her clothing and wrapped herself in an old thick dressing gown, but even it's warmth did little to halt the seeping cold that now spread through her body. In her bathroom, she ran a deep warm bath although she doubted she'd feel warm again for a long time. Her father's words had struck ice to her heart—they'd diminished the beauty of her night with Jack in a way she would never have believed possible.

She'd never in her life stopped to think of the true cost of her father's financial support of her over the years. It was galling to realise she had been as immature and empty as he'd so clearly pointed out. As she lowered herself into the bathwater, tears began to track down her cheeks.

She couldn't stay here anymore. She had to strike out, stand on her own two feet—somehow.

She must have dozed off in the bath because the distant peal of the telephone ringing made her jump, sending water rippling over the edge and onto the floor. The phone stopped and then in an instant started up again.

Lily levered herself up and grabbed a towel, wrapping it around her as she dashed into her bedroom to pick up the receiver before they hung up again.

"Hello?"

"Lily! Thank goodness you're still there. You have to come to FonCom, right now!"

Lily recognised her father's secretary's voice, although the woman sounded totally strung out.

"What is it? What's wrong?" Lily demanded.

"It's your father, I think he's had a stroke or something. He came into work all fired up, went into his office and about five minutes ago I heard this almighty thud. He'd collapsed on the floor. I called the ambulance, Lily, but he looks bad. You have to come, quickly!"

Sudden fear gripped at Lily's heart. Had she caused her father's collapse? He'd been so very angry before he'd left.

"Lily? Are you there?"

"I'm on my way."

She dropped the phone on the bed and ran to pull on some clothing—jeans, a T-shirt and running shoes—and, grabbing her car keys, flew down the stairs as fast as she could go.

The ambulance was outside FonCon's building when Lily pulled into the car park at the front. She raced from her car and through the front entrance toward her father's office.

"Here she is!" Charles's secretary came rushing toward Lily. "The paramedics are with him now, Lily, they're doing everything they can."

"Can I see him?" Lily tried to step past the other woman, to see into the office.

"Probably best to wait until they're ready to transport him. They've called the rescue helicopter. They think he's had a massive stroke. He'll need to go to Auckland City Hospital."

Lily sank into the nearest chair, her legs suddenly weak and unable to support her. Eventually the paramedics called Lily in. They'd stabilised her father as far as they were able and the helicopter's expected time of arrival in the FonCom car park was only ten minutes away. She was horrified when she saw the colour of her father's face and heard his laboured breathing through the oxygen mask.

"Will he be okay?" she asked the medic nearest her.

"That'll depend a lot on him, miss."

"He's a fighter, he won't give up." Lily had to believe it. As angry as she was with him, the prospect of losing him terrified her. He'd been the mainstay of her life.

When the helicopter arrived there was a flurry of activity as Charles was transferred to the aircraft.

"I'm sorry, miss, there won't be room for you on board. Can you get someone to bring you up to Auckland?"

"I'll bring her."

Lily spun around at the sound of Jack's voice and flew straight into his arms.

"I came as soon as I heard. Don't worry, it'll be okay," he consoled her, his strong warm hand rubbing up and down her back in a soothing motion. "Your father is as tough as they come."

Jack felt Lily's shoulders shake as sobs racked her body. He watched as the helicopter blades started spinning faster and faster until eventually the aircraft lifted off the asphalt and headed north.

"It's my fault, Jack. We had a terrible fight when I got home. It's all my fault."

He continued to rub her back. "No, Lily. It's not your fault. He hasn't been looking a hundred percent for a while, since long before you came home. Several people have commented on it, but you know your dad, he always believes he knows better."

Jack fought to keep a note of censure from his voice. It was the last thing Lily needed right now. A tiny pang of guilt hit him square in the chest. It wasn't the fight with Lily that had caused Charles Fontaine's collapse, of that he was certain. No, it would have been the final confirmation that the contract FonCom had been bidding for—the one guaranteed to pull them from the mire of debt Fontaine had gotten himself into in recent times—had been awarded to a rival company. It would have been the final nail in his coffin.

Jack realised just how literal that sounded and that pang grew stronger before he ruthlessly quashed it. There was no room for regret or remorse now. Had

Fontaine dealt reasonably with those around him, with the very people who'd catapulted his business onto the global stage in the first place, none of this would have been necessary.

He steered Lily toward his waiting car and helped her into the passenger seat. Her face was streaked with tears although the sobs had subsided into the occasional hiccough. He could see she was drawing on all the inner strength she possessed, trying desperately to pull herself together.

As he started to drive toward her home, she gave a cry of despair.

"What are you doing? This isn't the way to the highway."

"You'll need some things, Lily. He'll be in hospital for a while. It'll only take a few minutes for you to pack a bag, then I promise we'll be on our way."

She sank back in her seat, relief evident on her face.

"Thank you, I don't know what I'd have done without you. I can barely think straight, let alone drive my car."

"Hey, it's what friends are for, isn't it?" He reached over and took her hand, giving it a reassuring squeeze.

She gave him a wan smile in return.

At the house she packed the bare minimum of requirements. Jack called the housekeeper for her, giving the woman as much information as he'd been able to garner from Lily, and asked her to keep an eye on the house. Within twenty minutes they were on the road to Auckland.

"Why don't you try and get some sleep, hmm?" Jack suggested.

She looked exhausted. The demanding night, the

early morning and the stress now with her father had all culminated in a weariness that was visible in every line of her body.

"I'll try."

Jack sensed the moment she lost her grip on consciousness, felt the relaxation in her body as if it reached across the confines of the vehicle and touched him. She looked fragile, curled in the passenger seat of the Crossfire, the safety belt an inadequate cushion for her face. It would leave a mark, but he doubted she'd care.

He thought back to Charles Fontaine, to how the old man had looked as he'd been lifted into the waiting helicopter. Old, frail. Pity hit him hard, guilt even harder. He tightened his grip on the wheel. He had to rid himself of both. He'd planned this for a long time, Charles Fontaine's downfall. It was happening. The health issue was a sideline. He was only responsible indirectly. Fontaine had lived an unhealthy lifestyle for longer than Jack could remember. And he'd lived longer than his own father had had the chance to—Lily's father's abuses had been all of his own making. Jack forced his fingers to relax as the speeding car ate up the miles on the highway.

There was no room for pity or guilt in his life, only the satisfaction of seeing a job to its conclusion, and in exacting sweet revenge on both the Fontaines.

Thirteen

At the hospital, hours blurred into days, days into weeks. Lily lost track of time completely. Each waking moment was spent at her father's bedside as the specialist neurological team ran the gamut of diagnostic tests on her father. Each night she trudged from the hospital to a nearby motel where she tumbled into bed for a night of fitful sleep before returning again in the morning. Eventually, after a conference with a social worker and her father's medical team, a decision was made to transfer Charles to a palliative care facility in Onemata. There was little else that could be done once the final diagnosis had come in.

The stroke had caused irreparable brain damage. Essentially, Charles Fontaine was trapped inside a body that no longer functioned beyond the most basic of physical requirements. Lily wondered whether death would not have been more bearable, for him at least. She couldn't come to terms with how he seemed to have shrunk into a smaller version of the man who'd ruled her life. A man imprisoned behind frightened eyes that were glued each day to the door, waiting for her to arrive.

As aware as she was of her father's faults, and as much at loggerheads as they'd been the morning of his stroke—for most of her life—it was frightening to her to imagine a world without Charles Fontaine in it. Despite everything, he was her father and she loved him. In the long hours sitting at his bedside Lily had reached a level of peace in her heart over how he'd tried to rule and control her.

It would never be right, but she was certain, without doubt, that he'd been driven by love for her. It had been the kind of love that had driven her mother away from them both, as well as driven Lily to stay away as she had. But it was the only way he knew how to look after his own, and when push came to shove, he had looked after her, financially if not on the emotional level she'd needed.

She travelled with her father in the ambulance that was organised to transport him to the new facility, the journey undertaken at a vastly more sedate pace than her trip to Auckland with Jack two weeks ago. She hadn't seen or heard from Jack since the day he'd escorted her to the floor where her father had been admitted. She missed him with a physical ache that left her tired and lethargic.

After settling him in his new room, and promising she'd be back in the morning, Lily headed for home. As she came into the foyer of the building, her eyes scanned the cars lined up in the parking area beyond. She wished she'd thought to ask someone to bring her car up to the rest home. Come to think of it, was her car still at FonCom, or had someone taken it home for her by now? She reached for the courtesy phone on the wall to call a taxi.

"Need a ride?"

Jack's rich, deep voice was a salve to her soul. She spun on her heels. He edged himself up from where he'd been leaning against a pillar, his long legs encased in well-worn denim, a faded T-shirt stretched across his shoulders and his strong tanned arms bare. This was the Jack she remembered from her youth—the Jack she'd craved for the past two weeks. With a tiny cry, a mixture of joy and grief, she launched herself at him, arms outstretched.

Jack folded her against him. The warmth of his chest and the reassuring steady beat of his heart something solid she could cling to. And cling she did. She didn't realise she was crying until she felt his fingers slide across her cheeks. He tilted her face to his and he bent to take her lips. A gentle kiss, reassuring, comforting. Lily took the comfort and held it close, reluctant to break contact with him, with her sole rock of stability in uncertain waters.

Jack gently broke off the embrace.

"Come on. Let's get you home."

He bent to pick up the overnight bag she'd brought back with her. Lily silently nodded and slid her arm around his waist, her thumb hooked in his belt loop. It felt so right to be tucked under Jack's broad shoulder, the decisions she was going to have to face about her father's care seemed manageable with him by her side. Everything would be okay. Well, she corrected herself, as okay as it could get while her father still lived as he was now.

Briefly she wondered how things were at FonCom. She knew her father had kept a tight rein on things there, having overall control in all decision-making processes. She'd have to go in tomorrow to see how things were. Charles would expect it of her, and expect her to come back to him with the details, of that she was certain.

Mrs. Manson was leaving the house as they pulled up in the driveway.

"Ah, Lily." She greeted her with a grim smile. "I'm glad you're back. I need to speak with you about something quite urgent."

"Can it wait until tomorrow, Mrs. Manson? As you can see, I've only just arrived home," Lily replied as she walked toward the front door. Jack hung back at the car, watching, waiting.

"Actually, no, it can't. Until I'm paid, I won't be coming back to the house. If you could look into that for me and pay me what I'm due—" the woman flicked a sheet of paper in Lily's direction, forcing her to accept it "—then I'll be back as before."

Lily scanned the list. "Hold on a moment. You mean, you haven't been paid for a month?"

"That's what it says, doesn't it? I talked to your father before his stroke, and he was going to take care of it for me."

"I'm very sorry, Mrs. Manson. I'll see what I can find out tomorrow. Thank you for bringing it to my attention."

Lily rubbed at the worried frown on her forehead as Jack came toward her.

"Problem?"

"Yeah, Mrs. Manson hasn't been paid. Must be some glitch at the bank. I'll look into it tomorrow." Lily opened the front door and let herself into the house. "Come in, I'll put on some coffee."

"Sure, that'd be great, thanks."

As Lily walked down the tiled hallway to the kitchen it struck her anew how little like a home the house felt. She'd grown up here, surely she should have felt something when she came through the door. Home was supposed to be a place to retreat to, to relax in. She couldn't ever remember feeling that way. She glanced at the pristine rooms on either side of the hallway as she walked along, each one showroom-perfect and about as soulless as a magazine spread. No signs of the usual small things that made a house a home—an open magazine, an item of clothing, a forgotten glass on a tabletop. Nothing. With a thickening sense of dread, she knew she couldn't stay here alone.

She reached in the cupboard for the coffee beans but found the container empty.

"Sorry, looks like it'll have to be instant." She apologised as she fluttered about the kitchen.

She stilled as Jack reached across the granite countertop and put his hand on hers.

"Stop. Don't worry about it. Why don't you come back with me for a few days, this place feels like a mausoleum right now. Besides, if Mrs. Manson hasn't been paid, it's likely she hasn't been reimbursed for shopping, either. She'll have taken stuff home rather than leave it here, don't you think?"

"I didn't think of that." Lily spun around and checked the refrigerator, the pantry. Nothing perishable or vaguely edible remained. "What am I going to do?"

"Aside from the shopping?" Jack teased briefly. "No. Forget about it. Come back with me. Bring your car. I had it garaged here when I came back from Auckland. At least then you can come and go as you like. Okay?"

Lily worried at her lower lip with her teeth, then nodded. What he said made sense. "I won't be imposing on you, will I?"

"I want you with me. It's no imposition."

Lily watched as his eyes darkened and his lids lowered in a sultry look that promised she wouldn't feel alone for long.

"Then thanks, I accept. I'll get some more clothes and things."

"No problem. I'll get your car out of the garage and make sure everything's locked up behind me. Meet me out the front, okay?"

Later that night, with Lily sprawled naked across his chest, her legs entangled with his, Jack thought about what lay in store for her. The business with Mrs. Manson was just the tip of the iceberg. How much longer would it take before the ripples would reach earth-shattering proportions? Not terribly long, if his calculations were correct.

One thing still niggled at him. Their child. Had he yet succeeded in his final goal? Foisting a child bearing his name on Charles Fontaine's memory. An inner battle raged. His conscience ground incessantly at his need for satisfaction. A child deserved better than simply being a tool for settling an old score. Yet he knew any child of his would be loved unconditionally. It would bear his name with pride. It would know the love of his or her father as it deserved to from the point of conception.

He stroked a hand along the curve of Lily's hip and felt her press against him in response. The thought of her swollen with his baby sent a surge of longing through his body. He hadn't been oblivious to the faint silver lines across her hips, the telltale signs of weight gain, of stretched skin. The marks on her skin were the all that lingered of the child he'd been unable to track down even with the immeasurable resources at his disposal.

Gently he rolled Lily off his body and stroked her to wakefulness, his fingers deft on the points of her body that he knew without fail would bring her sighing to instant arousal. He would have his satisfaction against Charles Fontaine, he would have his child from Lily. Only then would the circle be complete.

"I don't understand it!" Lily threw her bag onto the couch in Jack's sitting room and flung herself into the chair.

"Don't understand what exactly?" Jack asked from where he stood at the kitchen tossing salad greens in a bowl.

From the outset it was clear that Lily was a stranger to the kitchen. In the interests of keeping them both healthy, they'd agreed he'd do the cooking each night when they weren't dining out.

"I had a meeting with Dad's second-in-charge today. He says staff are leaving in droves."

"Droves?" Jack raised an ironic brow.

"Okay, so I'm exaggerating. But several key staff have suddenly left, forfeiting holiday pay and benefits they've accrued. I can't understand it? So Dad's not at the helm anymore, but that shouldn't make a difference. The company should still keep running."

"Well, you can expect some instability. After all, your father always said he ran a tight ship." Except he'd run it so tight he'd strangled the lifeblood out of it, Jack thought as he watched Lily run her hand through her hair. The charming disarray it left in its wake spiked a fresh jolt of desire through his body. It seemed he couldn't get enough of her.

"That's not all. I went to the bank today, with a letter of introduction from Dad's solicitor as holding his enduring power of attorney. I know now why Mrs. Manson didn't get paid. There's no money in Dad's personal accounts. He's exceeded his overdraft limit by several thousand. It just doesn't make sense."

"You're right, that doesn't make sense." Jack set the salad on the small dining table off the kitchen and came through to the lounge. "But don't worry about it now. Tell me, how was your father today?"

Lily sighed and kicked off her shoes. "No worse, no better. It's about all I can expect, I'm told. It's awful seeing him like that. So helpless, so frightened. The nurses say that the only time he seems to relax is when I'm there. It's so hard."

Jack knelt in front of her and lifted one foot, massaging her instep and up to her ankles and calf muscles with sure, steady hands. Lily groaned with the pleasure of it.

"Hey, don't let it worry you. You do what you can, when you can. Right now, you need to eat."

"I couldn't eat, honestly. I haven't been feeling well all day. I think I might head upstairs and have a nap."

Jack looked at her in concern. "I'll take you to the doctor."

"No, I'm sure that's not necessary. I just need some sleep." She gave him a shy smile. "It's a commodity I've been lacking in lately."

"I'll have something light ready for you when you come back down," Jack promised, suddenly struck by how fragile she looked. There were shadows under her eyes and her cheekbones appeared even more defined than before, the hollows underneath them deeper.

Over the next few nights he reined in his hunger for her, allowing her the sleep her body craved and ensuring she had light, nutritious meals. It occurred to him that she'd been back now for just over a month, in fact, at the end of this week it was a month since they'd become intimate again. To his knowledge, she hadn't had a period yet. A thrill danced through his veins. Even though they had only been unprotected that one time, could she be pregnant?

As much as he wanted to force her to the doctor to find out for certain, he had to hold fire. It could just be a result of the emotional stress she was under on top of her slow recovery from the glandular fever. Add to that the disappointment she'd expressed at putting her business idea on hold, and it all combined to make sense that she was under a great deal of pressure.

He had to simply wait and hope, a fact that didn't settle comfortably with him at all.

Fourteen

Lily sat back in her father's chair and looked out of the second-storey window of the low-rise building that housed FonCom, staring at the manicured lawns, the staff tennis courts and pool, the nine-hole golf course.

Her father's empire.

He'd spent years building this up and had taken great pride in each new facility he'd been able to offer his staff. Each new toy a testament to the success of FonCom. Now the pool sat unused, the water discoloured and filled with leaves, the grass on the golf course too long to allow a decent game and the nets of the tennis courts sagged with disinterest.

She'd thought she couldn't be any more shocked than she had been after her visit to the doctor this morning. Sick and tired of feeling sick and tired every day, and fearful of a relapse, she'd made an appointment to see if they could get to the root of what ailed her. Finding out she was pregnant with Jack's baby had struck her dumb. How on earth would she tell him? Her mind had been whirling since she'd had the confirmation. Pregnant. As terrifying as it was, there was a part of her that sung with joy that they'd have another chance to be parents together. This time, she hoped with every beat of her heart, they could make it work.

How would she tell him? Lily played over several conversational starts in her mind but nothing felt right. She lay her hand over her belly. Another baby. And therein lay her answer. She had to tell him about Nathaniel. Only then could she give him this news as a salve to the child they'd lost.

She swivelled away from the view outside and forced her mind to concentrate on the reports she'd been given to go over by her father's financial team.

Two hours later she lifted her head. Today was proving to be one out of the bag of big shocks. Finding out about her pregnancy had been hard enough to believe, but not even that had affected her as deeply as the news that now spread out in front of her. Ripples of shock ran through her body as she tried to make sense of the reports.

Charles Fontaine had been operating in a downward spiral for some years and now stood poised on the precipice of total ruin.

Against the recommendations of his financial advisers he'd continue to expand and had borrowed heavily, determined that the next bid would secure a contract that would trade FonCom out of their problems. But the contracts had consistently gone to other companies and the debt had begun to mount up.

Even his home on the peninsula was mortgaged to the hilt, as was the company building—the mortgages held by a private finance company. In itself that raised a red flag to Lily's inexperienced mind. When a bank refused to lend any further funds, it was time to reassess, scale down, not to go looking for high-interest/high-risk loans from private lenders.

The management team had started to search the Companies Office record files in an attempt to secure the information Lily needed to make a personal plea to the mortgage holding company for a stay of execution. They felt that only a personal approach from her could possibly make any kind of difference at this point in time. It was that or shut the doors forever.

With careful optimism they'd projected that with cutbacks it was possible for FonCom to trade out of its difficulties—cutbacks and a whole heap of good luck. But without further extension on the overdue payments, they'd all be down the road. Correspondence to the mortgage holding company had elicited only a terse response making it clear that the directors would not consider any further delays before foreclosure. Now it was up to her.

Just how much had she contributed to her father's current financial mess? Lily wondered. For all the years he'd poured money into her accounts as she flitted from country to country and party to party in between contracts—spending up her earnings on clothing and airfares and using the generous allowance from her father to cover living costs—she owed it to him to make it right. To find some way to fight out of this disaster.

A knock at the door had Lily spinning around in the chair before rising to her feet. A sudden swell of nausea sent a fine sheen of perspiration beading on her upper lip and forehead.

"Miss Fontaine, are you all right?" her father's secretary, Jenna, asked as she came in.

"I'll be fine. Just stood up a little too quickly, that's all." But the nausea didn't abate, instead it rose in her throat, sending her in a mad dash for her father's private bathroom.

Once she was spent, Lily dashed cool water on her wrists and rinsed her mouth out thoroughly. Back in her father's office she sat in his chair as Jenna came bustling back in with a pot of tea. The scent of peppermint hung in the air.

"Here you are, you poor love. Try this. It's good for settling a squiffy tummy." She poured a cup of weak herbal tea in the bone-china teacup and handed it on its saucer to Lily.

Lily took a refreshing sip and leaned back in the seat. As the warm liquid slid down her throat she began to feel the soothing effects immediately.

"Thanks, Jenna. I don't know what came over me."

"You're running yourself ragged, my girl. Between spending hours with your dad and the time you've been locked in meetings here, no wonder you're not feeling well. Now make sure you finish that cuppa and call me if there's anything else I can do for you. Here's that

Companies Office search you were needing." Jenna passed the folder to Lily with a sharp look. "You're staying with Jack Dolan at the moment, aren't you?"

Lily felt a flush of colour rise in her cheeks.

"I don't believe that's any of your business, Jenna," she answered firmly. The woman might have worked for her father for years but she had no right to pry into Lily's personal business. Jenna was no fool. It wouldn't take her five seconds to put two and two together and come up with the right answer.

Clearly unruffled by Lily's comment, Jenna tapped on the cover of the folder. "Don't worry, Miss Fontaine. I won't be telling anyone, but remember, not much remains secret around here, young lady. Besides, you might want to reassess your accommodations when you read that."

Lily recognised the underlying warning in Jenna's words. It wouldn't be long before the whole town knew about the baby. After all, hadn't her father found out about her last pregnancy before she'd even had the chance to tell Jack? She leaned forward to open the file, sorting through the various papers that listed company names and details. It appeared the company that had loaned her father funds had been controlled by a cobweb of other companies, but with the information available via the Companies Office Web site it had been possible to track back through the complex array of ownership to one man.

Jack Dolan.

If Lily hadn't already emptied the contents of her stomach, she had no doubt she'd be doing it right now. Her skin felt as if it had suddenly grown too tight for her body and the hot rise of anger and betrayal boiled inside.

Suddenly she understood what Jack had been about. She closed her eyes and leaned back in the chair, the tone of his voice when he'd told her about Bradley Dolan's death ringing in her ears—the waves of resentment and frustration that poured off him even now. It all made sense. Jack had never been the kind of person to let things lie. He'd exacted his own revenge in the best way he knew how—by attacking her father at his heart, FonCom.

And now her.

She couldn't help but come to the conclusion that the rekindling of their love affair was a part of his scheme. Jack Dolan was not the kind of man who did things by halves. No, he'd have premeditated every last caress and she'd been stupid enough to fall in love with him all over again. And worse, fall pregnant to him again. She'd clearly played straight into his hands. No doubt Jack was laughing himself silly behind her back at the thought of how her father must feel, knowing she was with him.

She thought about the damage to FonCom. Hadn't he thought about the jobs that would be lost? The people whose lives would be affected much as his family's had been when his own father had lost his job? The sheer calculated coldness of Jack's actions sent a chill through her body.

Lily gathered up the papers in the folder and jammed them back into some semblance of order. She would face Jack with what he'd done. Only he had the power to undo it. She could only hope that he would be prepared to listen.

The house on the beach was silent as Lily let herself inside. She looked around the building that had so quickly come to feel like home and knew a pang of loss. Her relationship with Jack would never be the same after this. The burgeoning love she had for him now would never reach its rightful conclusion for as long as his hatred of her father fell between them.

Lily put the folder with the damning information from the Companies Office on the coffee table in the sitting room and pushed open the bifold doors to step out on the massive deck. She walked over to the railing and leaned against it. As she looked out over the sea she wondered if she'd ever find tranquillity in its view again after today, or if it would forever be imprinted with the taint of bitter betrayal.

How long she stood there she didn't know, but she knew the instant Jack arrived home. The hairs on the back of her neck prickled in early warning with the awareness that was intrinsic where he was concerned. She waited for his steady step on the wooden planks behind her before facing him.

"What's wrong? Is your father okay?" he asked, lifting a finger to stroke her cheek as he bent to kiss her.

Lily turned her head away, avoiding his caress.

"You have to ask *me* what's wrong? I'd have thought you knew exactly." She flung the words at him.

"You're talking in riddles. Something's obviously upset you. If it's not your father, what is it?"

She stalked inside the house, grabbed the folder of incriminating proof and thrust it at him when he followed her.

"What's this?"

"Open it." Lily crossed her arms across her aching chest. She could still barely believe the truth of it, the reality that he'd set her father up all along. Her fragile new world was crumbling around her.

Jack flicked open the folder and riffled through the pages, his lips settling into a grim straight line as he found the sheet with his name encircled in red pen. He lifted his head, his eyes meeting hers without any sign of regret in their depths.

"And the problem?" he asked coolly.

"So you don't deny it?"

"No."

He dropped the folder on the table and sat on the wide leather sofa, stretching his legs out before him and cupping his hands behind his head in a nonchalant pose that left Lily in no doubt he had no regrets about his activity.

She perched on the edge of the facing sofa.

"How long have you been undermining my father's business?"

"Does it really matter?"

"Yes, to me, it does, and I'm sure it does to all the people you're putting out of a job because of what happened to your father."

"They'll be compensated."

"Compensated? How? There's absolutely nothing

left for FonCom to compensate them with! They'll have no jobs, no security. How could you do that to them?"

"Them, Lily? Or your father? Or even you?" Jack suddenly snapped out of his comfortable lounging position and stood upright, tall and intimidating as he loomed over her. "Your concern for FonCom's staff does you credit, but it won't change anything. On my father's grave, Fontaine Compuware is going down."

The harsh purpose in his words seeped into her veins like poison.

"What happened to you, Jack?" Lily whispered. "Why this? Why now?"

"What happened? I told you what happened. Your father destroyed mine. I vowed I'd destroy him in return. As to timing, it'll be ten years next week since Dad died. Ten years since your father killed him. Fitting, don't you think?"

"Fitting? How can you even begin to think that? Since when has it been fitting to manipulate other people's lives like this? Okay, I can understand you're angry at my father, he was wrong in what he did. But this doesn't solve anything. It hurts people like your dad, people like your family."

"You're wrong. It does solve things. It settles the score for good. Your father won't be able to hurt anyone ever again."

"He already can't. He's never going to get better. If he finds this out, it will probably kill him."

"And you think that bothers me?"

"It should, of course it should."

"No, Lily. Your father made sure my family suffered.

He could have said anything when the police and the insurance company investigators questioned him about my dad's state of mind that day, anything but what he did. He led them to believe dad was suicidal when he was nothing more than a man stricken with fear that he could no longer support his family. Charles Fontaine stole my father's dreams and his ideas, and he made his millions on them. He deserves everything that's coming to him."

Lily slowly rose to her feet.

"You were never so bitter, Jack. I don't know you anymore. I can't believe you've let yourself become this person." Tears pricked at her eyes but she resolutely refused to give them freedom and blinked them back furiously. "You've lost your humanity."

Jack's cynical laugh was short. "Every last ounce of humanity I had left was buried with my father. I'm not going to apologise for what I've done, Lily. I swore on Dad's grave that Charles Fontaine would pay, and he has."

"Please, I beg you to reconsider. This anger, it's only going to eat you up, Jack. You have to give FonCom a chance to trade out of this. Give the staff a chance to keep their pride, their living."

"Eat me up? No, I don't think so. This is finally going to free me."

"So there's no way I can persuade you to give FonCom another chance?"

"As delectable as you are, no."

"Is that all I've been to you, Jack? A bit on the side while you bring my father down?"

"No. That's not all. I wanted to bring you down, too."

Lily froze. He what? She sank back on the seat on legs that were suddenly too weak to support her.

"Why?" she whispered. "What did I do to you?"

"You can sit there and ask me that? Your family has been the instrument of everything that brought pain to mine." Jack's voice rose in anger. "You took my child and you gave it away. You didn't even do me the courtesy of telling me we were going to be parents. I had to discover that when I started my investigations into your father's business affairs. How do you think it made me feel to find out you'd cast off my son or daughter without so much as a chance to bring the child up myself?"

"Stop it!" Lily cried. "You don't know what you're saying. I can't listen to this."

She staggered to her feet and dashed upstairs to the master bedroom and began dragging her clothes from the drawers and the wardrobe, jamming them haphazardly into the bag in which she'd brought them over. *He knew about Nathaniel!* He'd known all along. Suddenly the rekindling of their love affair took on a whole new and more sinister slant. Had it been his intention all along to get her pregnant again? She heard his footsteps at the door and looked up.

"Running away again?" His voice was cold, emotionless.

"No, I'm just giving myself some distance. I need thinking space and I can't do that with you. Not the way you are now—filled with anger and resentment. You have to let it go, Jack. It's poisoned you. I thought I knew you, thought I'd fallen in love with you again. But the man I love isn't the man here now. You're nothing but a stranger." She hefted the bag up by the shoulder strap and took a step toward the door. "Just tell me one thing."

"What is it?"

"Did you deliberately try to get me pregnant again, or was it just an accident?"

It took mere seconds for the truth to sink in and she watched as realisation swept through his mind.

"You're pregnant?"

"Apparently so."

"Have you told your father you're expecting my bastard? I bet he'll be thrilled with the news. I'm only sorry I won't be there to see the expression on his face."

"Don't you dare refer to this baby in those terms again. It's not a pawn in your filthy plans," Lily protested. Her hand flew to her stomach in an age-old gesture of protection. She was horrified that Jack could speak so harshly, it was a side of him she'd never known he was capable of.

"Like our last child wasn't a pawn in yours? You used that baby to get out of town, to make your father agree to you getting out from under his roof. I can't believe you just gave our baby up. Don't think I'll let you do that again." His face contorted, as if in pain.

"What makes you think I gave our baby up?" Lily fought to keep her voice level.

"I have the papers you signed, agreeing to a closed private adoption. Don't bother lying to me, Lily. You're just as ruthless as I am."

"Your information was out of date. He was never adopted out. Our son died."

Jack's heart hammered in his chest as her words sunk in. Dead? Their baby—*their son*—was dead?

"You're lying," he finally managed to say, pushing the words through lips that almost refused to form. "I saw the papers."

"My father forced me to sign those papers a few days after I rang you, when I begged you to come and get me. I believed him when he told me he'd offered you money to stay away from me, and that you'd accepted it."

"You believed him? You didn't even give me a chance to refute his lies!" Jack's fury boiled over.

"When had money ever not been important to you? All you ever spoke about was getting enough money to get out of Onemata to better yourself. Of course I believed him. He told me that without your support I'd be on my own and that our child would suffer for that if I didn't agree to the adoption. I had no choice—I had no way to support a baby on my own. I knew he would wash his hands of me, like I thought you had done. I had to give our baby a chance at a normal home—a normal family.

"You have no idea what I went through. I loved that baby with every beat of my heart. Every day of my pregnancy was a torment, knowing I'd agreed to give him away. Things progressed well, I was a textbook case for a perfect delivery of a normal healthy child, but there were complications during the delivery. There was a knot in Nathaniel's umbilical cord, it wasn't detected until it was too late. My labour was long, he was distressed, eventually the contractions cut off his oxygen. He was stillborn."

Her words, delivered in such a matter-of-fact manner, couldn't disguise the grief on her face. Pain such as he'd never known before pierced his chest. Even losing his father hadn't hurt this bad. All this time he'd imagined there was a child out there still, *his child.* He *wanted* to believe that was still the case and not what she had just told him, but the truth of her words was irrefutable. Speech failed him.

"I hope you're happy. You got what you wanted." Lily hefted her bag higher on her shoulder. "I'd like you to remember something though, before you close down FonCom completely."

"What?" He could barely speak, but forced the monosyllabic question from his mouth.

"If you think you're going to have anything to do with this baby, you can think again. There's no way on this earth that I'll let you within a hundred metres of us if you keep on with this cruel vendetta. And while you're thinking about it, remember this—your son or daughter will be born without a roof over its head because you destroyed its world before it was even born."

"You're not going anywhere with my baby."

"Just try and stop me. I will not let you taint this baby with your hatred and anger for past wrongs. You're just perpetuating the cycle. Worse, you're letting my father win because when push comes to shove, you're just like him. Win at all costs and damn the consequences and anyone else involved."

Jack stood back in shock as Lily swept past him. It wasn't until the front door slammed shut with a resoundingly hollow echo that he realised he should have stopped her.

Fifteen

Jack flew down the stairs and flung open the front door to the house in time to see Lily's car head out the driveway. He quickly grabbed his keys from the bowl at the front door and took off after her. She had a good head start but he knew his more powerful vehicle could catch hers.

Half way to his car Jack hesitated, slowing his steps to a complete stop. He watched her car disappear in the distance before going back up into the house.

Her final words to him battered inside his head, shouting down his silent insistence that she'd been lying to him about their son. About Nathaniel. His gut clenched. When they'd planned their future they'd hypothesised about potential names for the family they'd planned to have together. Nathaniel for a boy, Christina for a girl.

Jack sank onto one of his sofas and hung his head in abject misery.

What the hell had he done? Had it all been for nothing? He looked around at the trappings of his success. The home he'd built as a monument to his success and power in much the same way Charles Fontaine had done further up on the point. None of it would right past wrongs. None of it would bring his father back, nor would it turn back the clock and give his son another chance at life. Not a single dollar would repair the void that existed now between him and the woman he'd loved and lost and now loved again. And yes, he could finally admit to himself he loved her, had probably never stopped loving her. Why else had it felt so right to bring pleasure to her face, to share the things they'd both loved together? To hold her in his arms at night and know a peace he hadn't experienced in a decade?

It was galling to admit it, but Lily was right on so many levels. The harder he'd been driven to crush Fontaine, the more he'd become like him. Where had the gentleness gone in his life? The compassion? The sense of honour his own father had strived to imbue in his family.

He'd let it all slip away in increments, driven instead by the unhealthy need to conquer, which had become as detrimental to himself as it had been to the man he'd sworn vengeance against. Charles Fontaine had been integral in Bradley Dolan's death, but Bradley's reactions to his circumstances had been his own. Emotional? Yes. Ill-considered? Yes. He'd done what he'd done with his heart on his sleeve, as his wife had always teased him. If he'd taken the time to get legal advice, he may have found he was entitled to some restitution, instead he'd acted purely on feelings and they had led to his death.

Finally, Jack could begin to see his father as the man he was without the taint of Fontaine's influence. And in that he could see himself.

The past was exactly that. Past. It was time to step up to the plate and take responsibility. To look for another solution. A solution that would bring Lily back to his side forever. There'd be no half measures, no fumbles at the starting gate. This time would be for life. If he'd learned anything in the past few weeks, it was how much she still meant to him and how empty his life had been without her—a future without Lily by his side was inconceivable.

He got up and grabbed his laptop, flipping it open and pulling up the information he had on the FonCom loan. His fingers flew over the numeric keyboard as he considered various options until the sun sank below the horizon. Then, finally, he smiled. He had a plan. First, he wanted to see his baby's final resting place—he needed to close that door on the past before he could move on with an open heart.

Jack flipped open his cell phone and punched in Lily's number. The phone rang seven times before she answered—her voice sounded thick as if she'd been crying. His heart twisted in the knowledge he'd deliberately caused that pain.

He took a deep breath. "Lily?"

He heard her sigh on the other end before she answered. "What is it, Jack? If you're not prepared to tell me that you're going to grant FonCom an extension to trade out of their troubles, you can hang up right now. I will not discuss anything else with you until then. Is that clear?"

She had really toughened up since she'd come home. The old Lily Fontaine would never have stood up to him the way she had a few hours ago or the way she laid it on the line to him now. If anything, he found that one small change in her even more intoxicatingly attractive than before.

"Crystal clear. But before I agree to an extension, I need two things from you."

"So you'll agree to an extension?"

"On two conditions."

"What are they?"

He could hear the trepidation in her voice, sense her shoring up her defences against what he was certain she thought would be demands about the new life she carried.

"One, I need a detailed projection from FonCom's finance team as to exactly how they're going to meet the loan obligations. If it realistically looks promising, I'll consider interest-only payments for a set period. Once that time is up and the company's not in a position to repay principal as well as interest, I will be forced to foreclose."

"I'll let the management team know. No doubt they'll get back to you. What's the other condition?" Her tone of voice let out nothing about how she was feeling.

Jack took a deep breath. "I want you to show me Nathaniel's grave. Tomorrow."

"I can tell you where it is, surely you don't—"

"Those are my conditions, Lily. Take them or leave them. Each is dependant on the other."

"So if I don't show you?"

"All deals are off the table."

"Pick me up at FonCom at nine o'clock then."

She replaced the phone with a sharp click and he was left with the disconnected signal beeping in his ear. He wondered if he'd gone too far this time. Caution never had been his strongest trait. No, when the chips were down and the success of gaining what he wanted hinged on something as intangible as FonCom's future trading, he couldn't afford to take any risks. And he wasn't prepared to risk Lily, or their child, again. For anything.

Lily waited nervously in the foyer of the FonCom building. The early morning meeting with the heads of department had gone extremely well. They'd grasped the tentative lifeline offered by Jack with eager enthusiasm. She had no doubt that without Jack working against them in the background that FonCom would again work its way up to its previous position in the marketplace. Provided they could keep their current development team and put a stop to the unease among the remaining staff, there would be a strong future for all of them.

Her hand fluttered at her belly. Even for this unborn child there could be hope.

Lily saw Jack's Crossfire pull into the parking lot and she stepped outside to meet him. He'd alighted from the car and had come around to open her door for her. When he bent to kiss her, she turned her head and his lips settled on her cheek. She felt his lips pull into a tight smile.

"Lily." There was a warning note in his voice that made her look at him.

He immediately took advantage of her attention and pressed his lips against hers, coaxing them apart and tracing their inner softness with the tip of his tongue. Despite her anger at him, she couldn't hide her body's reaction to his touch—the flush of colour that swept up her throat—nor could she stop the tiny sound of longing that broke from her as his kiss deepened, demanding a response from her she ached to return. But she wouldn't give in. Not again. She wrenched her lips from his. As far as she was concerned, they lived on parallel planes, and until he was prepared to come down from his high road of vengeance and power, they'd never find a middle ground. She pulled back. A small satisfied smile played around his lips.

"You can wipe that smirk off your face, Jack Dolan. You might be able to drag a response from me, but it doesn't change who and what you've become. Don't think you'll get around me that easily."

"Don't worry. I won't underestimate you."

When he handed her into the car, Lily fought to control the flutters of nerves that danced across her spine. It was a good hour's drive to Auckland. In the close confines of the car, he'd be overwhelming.

"Where to?" he asked as he settled in the seat beside her.

"Purewa Cemetery."

He nodded in response and put the car in motion. Lily

tried to keep her gaze fixed on the scenery as they drove along the peninsula and finally drew onto the state highway that would lead them northward, but her eyes kept being drawn to Jack—to his hands as they competently handled the vehicle, to the length of his legs stretched out beside her, to the dark hair on his head so elegantly styled yet which could look so charming in disarray first thing in the morning.

Her thoughts cascaded in one direction then another as memory after memory of the past few weeks swamped her mind. She tried to push them back under control, but each tiny glimpse of the man she loved stole another piece of her heart as she tried to reconcile the quiet stranger sitting next to her with the lover she knew as intimately as she knew her own body.

His strength and power went way beyond the physical. His determination to get what he wanted at all costs evidenced by his destruction of her father's dreams. But underneath it all he was still the teenager she'd fallen in love with. The young man she'd pledged to love forever. The father of the child he'd never known. Lily couldn't help but hope that there was some way to bridge the yawning gap that now lay between them. But she'd learned to be realistic about hopes and dreams. They didn't always come true in the way you wanted.

By the time the car pulled in through the imposing entrance that marked the driveway to the Purewa Crematorium and Cemetery grounds, her stomach was tied in knots. Fine beads of sweat gathered on her upper lip and a swirl of nausea swept through her body.

Lily put her hand on Jack's thigh, her fingers tingling

at the hard heat that crept through the fine fabric and warmed her skin.

"Can you stop a minute, please?"

Jack gave her a swift glance before pulling in to the small car park at the administration block. He was around the side of the car and pulling open her door in a second and hunkered down next to her.

"You okay?" His sherry-gold eyes reflected none of the anger that had filled them yesterday, and only showed concern and care.

"Just a bit nauseous, that's all. Do you mind if we just wait a while before continuing?"

"I've waited this long. A few more minutes isn't going to be a problem." He straightened and rested his hand on the roof of the car. "Can I get you anything? Water? Something to eat?"

"No, truly. I'll be okay soon." She took in a deep breath. "There, I'm feeling better already. Shall we continue?"

Jack gave her a sharp nod. Tiny lines bracketed his mouth and he'd grown pale under his tan. It suddenly occurred to Lily how difficult this was for him. To have to come to terms with the truth about Nathaniel.

"It's beautiful there, in the children's area. Peaceful."

He nodded again, and she saw the muscles in his throat work as he swallowed. But still he said nothing. She directed him through the sweeping narrow roadways that wended through the cemetery, leading to the children's area of the gardens. The silence as the car engine died away was filled with the calls of birds high in the trees and the constant chirping of cicadas all around.

Lily opened her door and got out, Jack did the same.

He reached behind the driver's seat of his car and pulled out something small, concealing whatever it was in the breadth of his hand.

"Show me."

His words were an undeniable demand, but Lily sensed what this was costing him. His shoulders were a taut line, his spine tall and straight. She beckoned him over to the area where Nathaniel was laid to rest and bent to smooth away a few early falling leaves from the bronze plaque that marked the brief existence of their little boy.

Moisture pricked at her eyes as she read the words on the plaque even though she knew them off by heart.

Nathaniel, beloved son of Jack and Lily.

Always and forever in our hearts.

Jack dropped to one knee beside the tiny grave, his fingers running over the raised lettering before placing a small blue teddy bear on top of the marker. Lily fought to hold back the tears that choked her as she watched his strength crumble. Watched as his shoulders began to shake and his head dropped in unmistakeable grief, his hand across his eyes.

Without thinking, she reached across and wrapped Jack in her arms, holding him as tight to her as she could. Offering, unreservedly, comfort in the storm of his anguish. Jack clung to her like a man drowning, but eventually she felt his breathing begin to calm, and he pulled away from her.

His face was tight, like a mask. Skin stretched over his cheekbones, his lips pressed hard together in a straight line. His eyes filled with lost memories.

"I will always hate your father for what he's done, Lily. He cheated us both."

"I know, but he's my father. He'll always be my father. We've all made terrible mistakes. We have to let go of them or the wrongs rule us and our lives. There's no future without forgiveness."

"I can't forgive him for this." Jack gestured toward the grave.

"I know."

"From the time I found out about your pregnancy, all I could think about was someone else was raising our baby. I was so angry—felt so cheated. I would have moved heaven and earth to be with you if I'd have known. You stole that from me by not telling me, Lily. You still had a choice, even after signing the consent form, of letting me know the truth. But you didn't even do that."

Lily wrapped her arms tight around her, suddenly cold in the dappled late summer sun. He was right. She should have tried to contact him.

"I know. And I have to live with that. I wanted to call you again, but I lacked the courage. I was so frightened. It was easier to give up. I persuaded myself that Dad had been right, that you didn't want anything to do with me." She walked over to a nearby bench seat and sat before continuing. "I still don't know how Dad found out about the baby—I think one of the staff at the doctor's surgery must have told him. The day he sent me away, I'd never seen him so angry or so controlled. He told me exactly what was going to happen. I had no choice in the matter. I argued with him. I told him that we were going to be together, that we were in love. But he wouldn't listen.

"He had a driver waiting to take me to Auckland where he'd arranged for a family to care for me until the baby was born. They looked after me, but on my father's terms. Dad only came up to see me the once, to get me to sign the adoption consent. After that, he would ring me once a week. I used to beg him for news of you. He refused to talk about you, said you'd moved on with your life and it was time for me to do so, too. Eventually, I convinced myself I'd done the right thing by agreeing to the adoption.

"When Nathaniel was stillborn I couldn't bear to go back to Onemata. Dad made it easy for me to keep running from my mistakes, feeding me money to keep me overseas, and I let him."

"It wasn't all your fault, Lily."

"No, maybe not. But I perpetuated the lie. I chose to stay away until I virtually self-destructed. I can't do that anymore." She stood and walked over to Jack, laying her hand on his chest. "I came home to face my fears—how I felt about you was my biggest. You made me fall in love with you all over again, Jack. And I let you. I wanted to love you with all the passion we had before, and more. I welcomed you into my heart and into my body, and we've been given a second chance.

"Losing your father that way was wrong. What my Dad did to him was wrong. I can see why you did what you did to Dad, to FonCom. But answer me this, Jack. Was it worth it? We've all been victim to my father's manipulation, but there comes a point where we have to move forward, take back control, make a new life. I'm willing to do that with you, if you're willing to take the risk."

She reached up and cupped his jaw with her hand. "We had a great love once. We can't have that same love back, but we can start again. The only way we'll ever heal is if you let go and forgive. Forgive my father, forgive me, forgive yourself."

Her words struck deep into the ice that encased his soul, layer by layer peeling away the shrouds of anger and resentment that had driven him to succeed. The bitter aftertaste of revenge lay thick on his tongue.

"You're right, vengeance hasn't given me back what I expected or wanted. The only thing that can do that is having you back in my life so we can live those dreams we started. I can forgive you, Lily, and maybe in time I can forgive myself. Your father, that's going to take some time." He cupped his hand against her belly. "For years I let the things I hated in life drive me, and yes, I'm successful. But in comparison to this—" he pressed gently against her "—it's all been for nothing if we don't have a future together, all of us. I love you, Lily Fontaine. I will always love you. I want to marry you, Lily. Will you be my wife, share my home and my future? Help me be the man you deserve?"

For a minute he was unsure of her response, her eyes remained clouded for an infinitesimal moment before clearing. His heart began to beat faster as she pressed one of her hands over his and with the other drew his face down to hers.

"Nothing in this world would please me more."

"Can I take that as a yes, then?"

"Yes, oh yes!"

When she opened her mouth to him this time there

was no holding back, no reluctance. He wrapped his arms around her and cradled her body against his, where she belonged. Where she'd always belonged. For the first time, in what felt like forever, Jack felt his father's approval for what he'd done whisper over him like the soft summer breeze that teased the air around them.

It was time to move forward with a clean slate—together, forever, stronger than before.

* * * * *